P9-DGB-149

A novel based on the major motion picture

Adapted by Ann Lloyd

Based on the screenplay by The Wibberleys

Story by The Wibberleys & Ted Elliott & Terry Rossio

Based on characters created by Jim Kouf and Oren Aviv & Charles Segars

Produced by Jerry Bruckheimer, Jon Turteltaub

Directed by Jon Turteltaub

DISNEP PRESS

New York

·Special thanks to John Sabel

If you purchased this book without a cover, you should
be aware that this book is stolen property. It was reported
as "unsold and destroyed" to the publisher, and neither
the author nor the publisher has received any payment
for this "stripped" book.

Copyright © 2007 Disney Enterprises, Inc.

All rights reserved. Published by Disney Press, an imprint of Disney Book Group.
No part of this book may be reproduced or transmitted in any form or by
any means, electronic or mechanical, including photocopying, recording, or by any
information storage and retrieval system, without written permission from the
publisher. For information address Disney Press, 114 Fifth Avenue,
New York, New York 10011-5690.

Printed in the United States of America

First Edition
1 3 5 7 9 10 8 6 4 2

Library of Congress Catalog Card Number: 2007904361
ISBN-13: 978-1-4231-0627-2
ISBN-10: 1-4231-0627-X

This book is set in 14.5-point Centaur MT

Visit nationaltreasure.com

PROLOGUE

Washington, April 14, 1865

On the streets of Washington, D.C., children darted among crowds, sparklers in hand. Men and women, smiles on their faces, meandered about, taking in the sights and sounds of the celebrating throngs. The Civil War was over! The soldiers were returning! Peace was restored at last!

But not everyone was celebrating. Ignoring the festivities, a well-dressed gentleman tied his horse to a post outside a small tavern. Satisfied his mount was safe, the man turned and scanned the area, his eyes coming to rest on someone in decidedly worse shape than he was. A disheveled man, his eyes cold, leaned against the wall of the tavern. Raising his hand, the well-dressed gentleman pointed at the other man's shirt. A gold pin flashed in the light of the sparklers before the man quickly buttoned up his coat, concealing the item. Then, in silence, the two entered the tavern.

Inside, the atmosphere was a bit more subdued. A piano player tickled the keys, playing a now familiar Union anthem, while behind the bar, the barkeeper read a newspaper, unconcerned by the newest patrons. In the back room, equally unconcerned with his surroundings, a bespectacled man by the name of Thomas Gates sat, immersed in his studies. His nine-year-old son, Charles Carroll Gates, sat at his side, fidgeting.

Suddenly, a pair of shadows covered Thomas's books. Looking up in annoyance, Thomas found himself staring into the eyes of the well-dressed man and his companion.

"They say you got a mind for conundrums and such," the gentleman said in way of greeting.

"He's the best," Charles piped up, his voice full of pride.

Shooting the child a stern look, the gentleman

pulled a leather-bound diary from his pocket and placed it on the table. "We got something we were hoping you could take a look at."

Thomas glanced at the open page of the diary, his eyes quickly scanning the words. But before he could speak, Charles exclaimed, "That's a Playfair cipher!"

Holding back a groan, Thomas reached into his jacket and produced an unlit sparkler. Handing it to his son, he ordered him outside. But not before giving him a stern warning. "Try not to burn down the Capitol. They just built it." When Charles was safely out of the room, Thomas turned his attention back to the two men. "That cipher's impossible to decode without the key," he explained.

The gentleman pointed to the page. "I believe what you need is right here."

Thomas looked back down at the book, his eyes darting between the cipher and the phrase the man had alluded to. The gentleman knew that look—Thomas was interested. And interested was exactly what he wanted. "So? Can you decode it?"

"It'll take some time," Thomas answered.

The gentleman checked his pocket watch. His

friend noticed and said to him, "Go on. I'll meet up with you later."

As the man pushed his way past the long bar, the barkeeper looked up. "I know you," he shouted. "You're that actor fella, aren't ya?"

With a smile, the gentleman acknowledged the recognition. But his expression changed upon hearing the barkeeper's next words.

"Well, you'll never be the actor your father was," the man announced.

"Perhaps," the gentleman replied through clenched teeth. "But I will soon be the most famous." And with that, he pushed his way out the door, jumped on his horse, and disappeared into the crowded streets. He had an appointment to keep.

Moments later, the gentleman arrived in an alley behind one of the city's theaters. Handing the reins of his horse to a young stagehand guarding the door, he slipped into the back of the building. Inside, the faint sounds of the actors' voices could be heard as they played out a scene from the popular play, *Our American Cousin*. But the man did not stop to notice. He kept moving, climbing up a steep flight of steps that led to one of the theater's boxes—the esteemed State Box, to be specific. When he arrived at the top, he handed a note to a valet who let him pass. Walking over to the door, his heart began to pound in his chest. Through a small peephole in the door, the man could see President Lincoln and his wife, Mary Todd, sitting next to Major Rathbone and his fiancée, Clara Harris. It was just as he had planned. Smiling, the gentleman pulled out a derringer from his pocket.

Silently, he slipped into the box, his finger on the trigger. Laughter erupted in the theater, giving the man his chance. He aimed at the president and pulled the trigger. The shot rang out, loud and true. Leaping to his feet, Major Rathbone rushed to the president's aid, but pulling a knife, the shooter swiped at Rathbone, slicing his arm. Before the major could recover, the man stepped out onto the railing of the box seats and jumped. But as he did so, his boot spur caught on the American flag draped across the front of the seats. Awkwardly, he fell to the stage.

As all around him screams rang out and people ran for safety, the man stood up, a knife in his hand. "*Sic semper tyrannis!*" he shouted in Latin. The phrase meant, "Thus always to tyrants." And, turning, John Wilkes Booth, the man who would forever be known as Lincoln's assassin, limped offstage while behind him the theater burst into chaos.

Back at the tavern, Thomas was busy deciphering the coded message. He was scribbling on paper, trying to put together the words to unlock the mystery. Unbeknownst to him, Charles was hiding behind the door, watching everything.

Thomas stared at the words he had jotted all over his paper and finally scribbled down the decoded message: GOLD FOR CONFEDERACY. Thomas's eyes narrowed. "This is a treasure map!" he cried. Looking up, his eyes fell on the disheveled man's open jacket. The pin, hidden until now, flashed in the candlelight. With sudden clarity, Thomas realized exactly who he was dealing with. "KGC . . . you're Knights of the Golden Circle."

The stranger calmly took a gun out of his coat and pointed it at Thomas. "I'd much appreciate it if you would finish deciphering that code now," he said.

Suddenly, the door to the tavern flew open and

a man rushed in, his cheeks flushed and his eyes wide. "The president's been shot!" he cried.

As people rushed out to see what was going on, Thomas reached out and grabbed for the diary—at the same time the other man did. For a moment, both men struggled, tugging and pulling the book between them. But then, a shot rang out and Thomas fell back, ripping a handful of pages from the diary. He had been shot!

"Dad!" Charles cried, darting out of his hiding spot and rushing to his father's side. "Dad!" he cried again, as his father collapsed into a chair near the fireplace.

"The war is over," Thomas said, his gaze steely behind his spectacles. Flicking his wrist, he dumped the diary pages into the roaring fire.

Letting out a groan, the disheveled man scrambled over to the fireplace and reached his hand in, ignoring the heat. Quickly, he fished out one burning page and patted it out. When the page was safe, he looked back at Thomas. "You're wrong about that," he said. "The war has only just begun." Clutching the page, he scurried out of the tavern.

In his chair, Thomas felt himself grow weaker.

Turning toward his son, he spoke his final words. "The debt," he coughed, "that all men pay . . ."

Meanwhile, in a prison cell in Fort Jefferson, the man, known as Michael O'Laughlen, who had shot Thomas Gates, now sat, a convicted conspirator in Lincoln's assassination. He faced an uncertain future, but he did not care. Alone in his cell, he slipped a half-burnt diary page from the hem of his pants.

It was the page from Booth's diary. O'Laughlen smiled. Booth's secrets would go to the grave . . . with O'Laughlen.

CHAPTER ONE

Fort Jefferson, Dry Tortugas
Seventy miles west of Florida, present day

Standing on the deck of his research vessel, Benjamin Franklin Gates looked out at the ruins of what had once been Fort Jefferson. The Florida sun beat down on the crumbled brick and made the water that surrounded the island sparkle. But Ben wasn't seeing the beauty of the day. His mind was on more important things—namely, historical treasure. Turning, Ben crossed the deck, a tank of oxygen in each hand. While it looked as if he hadn't shaved in days, his eyes were filled with excitement, and the wet suit he was wearing was most likely why. He was going to see some action.

Unfortunately, not everyone appeared as happy. Abigail Chase, Ben's fiancée, followed him, her arms crossed across her chest.

"Ben, we've been diving for a week. When are you going to admit you might be wrong?" she asked, barely containing her annoyance.

Ben didn't even look up. "When I'm wrong . . ." He continued to prepare for the dive, handing one of the tanks to another diver, Zach, who was checking the gear. ". . . which I'm not. Why else would someone risk making an unscheduled trip in the middle of hurricane season?" He zipped up his wet suit.

"They were likely bringing emergency medical supplies," Abigail argued. "Half the prison population was dying of yellow fever."

"Including Michael O'Laughlen," Ben pointed out. "That's why the Knights of the Golden Circle were so desperate to get to him."

Abigail stared at the handsome man, her eyes pleading. "Ben, there's never been any evidence that the Knights of the Golden Circle were linked to the conspirators."

Ben finally met Abigail's gaze and smiled. "Not yet." He leaned over and gave her a kiss. With the sun streaming down on her blonde hair, she looked quite beautiful. Then, taking a deep breath, he dove.

As Ben tumbled into the water, Abigail sighed. Although she hated to admit it, Ben's hunches were usually correct. After all, he had been right about the treasure map on the back of the Declaration of Independence. *And* the Templar Treasure. When they first met, Abigail had been wary of Ben and his all-consuming interest in history. But somewhere on the way to finding the National Treasure, Abigail had fallen madly in love with him—crazy history buff or not. She just wished he wasn't *so* stubborn. . . .

Underwater, Ben surveyed the area. His eyes fixed on the wreckage of the cargo steamer that had drawn them to this particular spot in the ocean. There was a team of divers working on the site, the area lit up by large klieg lights. With smaller lights on their helmets, Ben and Zach made their way into the steamer hold, swimming down a dark, narrow corridor.

"With all due respect, Dr. Gates," Zach said into his radio, "we have searched every inch of this ship."

Ben hit the button on his radio. "I had an epiphany last night. . . ." He stopped to swing a light onto two wagon wheels and several crates. "Sometimes these steamers were used to smuggle goods during the Civil War."

Swimming slowly, Ben knocked along the bottom of the hull until he heard the distinct thud of a hollow spot. Pulling out a small hammer, Ben began to chip away at the coral that covered the hull. After a few moments, the debris cleared to reveal a handle. The years of being undersea had rusted the latch shut, so Ben took a cutting torch from his belt and worked at the hatch. When he was finally able to open it, they found a large metal strongbox. Ben and Zach shared a smile.

As the two divers grabbed the metal box, the ancient ship shifted, throwing their balance off. The handle of the box slipped from Zach's grasp, sending his end crashing down . . . right into a steel beam! As the two men watched in horror, the beam snapped, and the ship let out a giant groan. Before they knew what was happening, Ben and Zach were tossed against the hold's wall, landing several feet apart. A moment later, the beam fell on top of Zach, pinning him to the ground.

"I can't move!" he shouted in panic.

Quickly scanning the area, Ben caught sight of an iron bar. Using it as leverage, he tried to lift the beam. But it was too much for the rusted instrument. The bar snapped and the ship shifted once again. In that moment, a piece of debris cracked Zach's helmet and he started to lose air.

"Abigail, I need you to drop the Zodiac," Ben said into his radio calmly.

Up on the ship, Abigail panicked but did as Ben asked. Throwing the large block of rubber overboard, she watched it sink beneath the waves. Then she waited.

Below the surface, Ben guided the Zodiac to fit under the beam that had pinned Zach. When Ben pulled the cord, the Zodiac inflated into a raft and lifted the beam up. With the help of other divers, Ben was able to get Zach free and up to the boat before he lost consciousness.

When they were all safely on deck, Abigail leaned in to Zach. "How do you feel? Are you hurt?" she asked.

But Zach was watching the water, unaware of the beautiful blonde beside him. Suddenly, the water bubbled and churned as the box that had caused all the trouble broke the surface. Smiling, Zach turned to Ben. "Does this mean we're all getting A's, Dr. Gates?"

Ben looked over at Abigail, and smiled. "He's fine."

As soon as the box was on deck, Ben leaned over and began to drill. A moment later, he lifted the top to find silt and sand. Not to be discouraged, Ben sank his hands deep into the box, and began to feel around. When he pulled his hands out, they held a handful of coins.

"Nineteenth-century Liberty Head gold coins," Abigail said.

"To bribe the guards," Ben concluded.

"It's just a theory," Abigail replied matter-of-factly.

Ignoring his fiancée, Ben continued to search the box. Next he pulled out a small metal cigarette box. Inside was a rusted pewter stickpin. Ben wiped the rust off the pin and saw the circular emblem, which looked like a peace sign with horizontal lines going across the circle.

Looking once again at Abigail, Ben grinned. "KGC pin," he declared.

★   ★   ★

A short while later, the sound of a helicopter filled the sky. Back on the dry ground of Fort Jefferson, Ben and Abigail looked up from their work to watch as the chopper landed on the grassy area by the research camp. They walked over to meet a man—Dr. Nichols—as he climbed out of the chopper.

"Where is it?" he asked, by way of greeting. "Show me!"

Ben held up the pin, and Nichols's eyes grew wide. "See the *K* here," Ben said, pointing. "And the *G* and the *C*."

"Knights of the Golden Circle," Dr. Nichols said, a grin spreading across his face. "So, who here's going to help me unload this case of champagne?" he asked excitedly.

But Abigail was not so quick to celebrate. "This doesn't prove that the KGC was behind Lincoln's assassination."

"Abigail, come on," Ben said, as he popped open a bottle of champagne. "What's it going to take for you to admit I was right?"

Abigail sighed. She and the world were going to need more proof than a stickpin before anyone believed that the KGC was part of the Lincoln assassination.

CHAPTER TWO

Since Ben had discovered it deep beneath New York City, the Templar Treasure—and Ben along with it—had become a huge draw for Washington, D.C. Ben was pleased to see the interest the exhibit was getting and was more than happy to give the required lectures to the audiences of tourists, historians, and wannabe treasure hunters who flocked to the museum.

Today, inside one of the museum's seminar rooms, a banner with the words, THE CIVIL WAR—CIVILIAN HEROES, lined one wall. Standing on a dais, with Dr. Nichols behind him, Ben addressed a room full of historians and amateur treasure hunters. But this was not a speech about vast treasure. It was about something much closer to Ben—his ancestors.

"The Knights of the Golden Circle was a Southern extremist group operating in the North to subvert Union efforts," he said, pausing before he went on. "Had Thomas not burned those pages that night, the KGC may have gotten their hands on that gold, and the Union may very well have lost the Civil War."

Before Ben could go on, an audience member raised his hand.

"You expect us to believe that the missing pages of the Booth diary were actually burned by your ancestor because they contained a treasure map to a cache of Confederate gold?" the man asked.

"Actually," Ben confided, "it was a secret message leading to the map, not the map itself."

"Did Charles Gates ever come forward with this information after Lincoln's assassination?" another man asked.

As Ben was about to answer, the room filled with the sound of "Yankee Doodle." With an embarrassed grin, Ben glanced down at his now ringing phone and gave a silent groan. The caller ID read: "Herney's Movers." This could not be good.

Turning his attention back to the crowd, he introduced his father, Patrick Gates. The older man had become his strongest ally ever since helping him discover the Templar Treasure, and they now often made presentations together. It was a nice change from the years of awkwardness that had previously existed. And it meant that Patrick could handle the room while Ben dealt with his still-ringing phone.

Moving off the stage, Ben answered the call. "Hello," he said, not bothering to hide his annoyance.

"I'm at the house," the mover's gruff voice said, "and there's a lady here sitting in one of the chairs you have tagged for us to move."

The "lady" he was referring to was none other than Abigail and the "house" was the large estate that, up until very recently, they had lived in together. But after the excitement of the Templar Treasure discovery had faded and Ben had become increasingly distracted by new treasures to be found, Abigail had grown tired. The man she had fallen in love with and even agreed to marry was not the same anymore. The most recent trip to Fort Jefferson had been the last straw. And so, she had split up with him.

Which meant their belongings now had to split as well.

"She won't let us take it," the mover went on, causing Ben to stifle a growl of rage. He could just imagine Abigail sitting sternly in the chair, her arms crossed. He did not have time for this—and she knew it. After a few more minutes of bickering—with the mover as the go-between—Ben gave up. Abigail could have the chair. He just wanted to get back to his lecture. Flipping the phone shut, he walked back onto the stage just in time to hear Dr. Nichols ask if there were any last questions.

In the back row, a man in his forties stood up and raised his hand. His face was strong and confident and he looked every inch the respectable business-man—down to the briefcase by his side. Making sure he had Ben's attention, he asked in a clear voice, "What do you think ever happened to that Booth diary page? The one Michael O'Laughlen snatched out of the fire that night?"

"We'll likely never know. The secret died in prison with Michael O'Laughlen," Ben answered.

"Perhaps," he said as he began to make his way forward, a smile on his face. "Perhaps not." When he reached the stage, he went on. "You see, I have one of those great-great-granddaddies just like you do, by the name of Silas Wilkinson. I'm Mitch Wilkinson."

As Ben, Patrick, and Dr. Nichols looked on, with the rest of the audience also entranced, Mitch dialed a combination on his briefcase and continued to speak. "Silas used to tell a story about the night Lincoln was killed. He worked at the tavern where Booth and O'Laughlen met with a group of men, one by the name of Thomas Gates."

At the mention of their ancestor, Ben and Patrick exchanged a look. Where was Mitch going with this story?

"You see, as Silas tells it, Booth didn't seek out Thomas Gates regarding a treasure map that night." He waited a beat. "It was Thomas Gates who called the meeting. A KGC meeting."

Gasps could be heard in the room as the audience took in the significance of such a statement. Heads swiveled from Mitch to the Gates men.

"That's ridiculous!" Patrick shouted.

Everyone turned back to Mitch as he took in Patrick's outburst. He seemed unbothered. "Silas said the men had an argument. Guns were drawn.

Thomas was killed. One of the men tore some pages out of the book, threw them in the fire . . . but . . ." Mitch popped open the suitcase and pulled out a weathered piece of paper sealed in plastic. As he held up the paper, the crowd quickly saw the telltale burnt markings that could mean only one thing. ". . . One of the missing Booth diary pages," Mitch confirmed. "Which I've come to turn over to the museum."

And with that the room erupted, while Ben, Patrick, and Dr. Nichols stood in shocked silence.

A short while later, the four men stood in the now empty exhibition hall. An uncomfortable silence had descended upon the room as Ben, Patrick, and Dr. Nichols examined the burnt page.

Despite the age of the paper, the date, April 12, could clearly be seen as could a list of names corresponding with a Latin phrase. Ben's eyes ran down the list, and then hovered at the end, where one name stood out: Thomas Gates—*artifex*.

Dr. Nichols looked down the list before breaking the silence. "Surratt—*copiae*?" he asked.

"'Military supplies,'" Mitch answered. "Mary

Surratt was convicted and hanged for supplying Booth with a rifle and field glasses."

"'Thomas Gates, *artifex*,'" Ben hissed, his eyes never leaving the paper.

Mitch had a ready answer for that listing as well. "Latin for 'designer' or 'mastermind' . . . he planned the assassination."

"It could mean mastermind of anything!" Patrick fumed. Pointing at the charred edge of the page, he added, "It's burned off right there."

His father's words ringing in the air, Ben finally looked up and locked eyes with Mitch. "Why wasn't this given to the authorities after the assassination?" he asked, trying to keep his voice steady.

"There were powerful men at that KGC meeting, men high up in the government," Mitch answered. "Silas didn't know whom to trust. Then I heard about your story, so I went and dug the page out. I thought maybe I'd find myself a treasure map. Instead, I found the name 'Thomas Gates' written on it."

"Thomas Gates was a patriot," Patrick declared. "He would've never plotted to assassinate the president."

As the other three men argued over whose family

was lying, Dr. Nichols continued to stare at the burnt page. Reaching out a hand, he indicated that he would like to see it. Mitch handed it over and watched out of the corner of his eye as Dr. Nichols moved toward the display case that held the infamous Booth diary. The sound of the case creaking open caught the attention of Patrick and Ben, who now turned to watch as Nichols lined the burnt page up to the ripped one in the diary. It was a perfect match!

Patrick let out a groan as Ben put a hand to his heart.

"Of course, it'll have to be tested thoroughly to authenticate it," Nichols said, trying hard to sound reassuring.

But it was no use. The Gates name was once again in jeopardy.

CHAPTER THREE

In another part of D.C., customers wandered through a popular bookstore, browsing the crowded shelves. But at the table where Riley Poole sat, there was not a soul around. The young man's head was bowed over a crossword puzzle, his eyes focused behind his thin-framed glasses. He looked every part the successful author—minus the fans. Riley was there to promote his new book, *The Templar Treasure and Other Myths That Are True*. Unfortunately, the signing was not well attended, and so he found himself doing a crossword puzzle instead of autographing books.

A woman wandered over and saw the sign on the table highlighting the Templar Treasure. Her eyes lit up, and she turned her attention to Riley. "The author's here? Signing copies?" she asked.

Riley looked up proudly. "Yes, I'm the author."

"You are?" the woman said, a note of disbelief in her voice.

"See?" Riley said, pointing to his name. "Riley Poole. That's me."

"I thought that guy Benjamin Gates found the treasure," she said, clearly disappointed.

"Well, yes," Riley told her. "But I assisted him."

The woman was not impressed—especially when Riley informed her that he had published the book himself. Riley sighed and watched the woman walk away. When a beautiful young college girl rushed over, he felt a bit better.

"Ohmigosh!" she cried. "Are you Ben Gates?"

Without missing a beat, Riley replied, "Yes, yes, I am."

"Do you own a red Ferrari?" she asked.

Riley puffed up his chest. This was promising. "Yes, I do," he replied.

"I think it's being towed," the girl said, gesturing to the window.

His face fell. Of course. This was just the icing on

the stale cake. With a sigh, he got up, left the store, and began the long walk home.

A while later, Riley arrived at his apartment to find Ben sitting on his front step.

"Ferrari in the shop?" Ben asked with a teasing smile.

When Riley explained that the IRS had impounded it, Ben pointed out that he should have paid his taxes.

"I have!" Riley exclaimed. "Do you know what the taxes are on five million dollars? Six million dollars. Especially after your tax man sets up a corporation for you on an island that doesn't exist and assures you that that's how rich people do it. Then you get audited and slapped with a huge fine . . . with interest!"

Ben waited for his friend to finish ranting. Then he simply said, "I need your help."

"Does it involve treasure?" Riley asked, hopefully.

Later that night, Riley found himself sneaking onto the grounds of a New England manor, Ben by his side. After his friend had filled him in on Mitch Wilkinson and the recently revealed letter, Riley had been more than happy to help. Plus, it wasn't like his social calendar was jammed. Now both men were crouched down as they made their way as silently as possible across the wide, dark lawn. Reaching the side of the house, Ben peeked through a dark window.

"Can't you just ask Abigail to help?" Riley asked from his spot beside Ben.

It wasn't an odd question. After all, the house they were outside of was Ben's—or at least it had been.

"Not only did she change the locks and alarm codes," Ben answered, "she won't talk to me."

Gesturing to each other, the two stepped away from the window and made their way to the front porch. It was time to get to work. Slipping off his trusty backpack, Riley rummaged around inside until he found what he was looking for—an eight-piece lock-pick set. Placing it on the ground, he chose the necessary tool and got to work. As he played with the lock, he continued his conversation with Ben. "What happened between you two?" he asked. He had liked Abigail and Ben. They made sense together.

"I don't know. She started using the word 'so' a lot," Ben said. He grew silent as he thought about the countless arguments and fights that had started with that one little word.

Unaware of his friends inner musings, Riley kept working on the lock. "Maybe getting to know someone in the midst of a historic treasure find is not the best way to determine compatibility."

Click!

The door unlocked, giving Riley thirty seconds to enter the house and disable the alarm. He jumped up and ran into the main hall. Within eight seconds he had bypassed the alarm.

"That's why I always tell people to get a dog," Riley explained.

Not bothering to debate the pros and cons of dog ownership, Ben rushed into the room he had once used as a study. Walking over to the desk he began searching through the drawers. Finally, he found what he was looking for—Abigail's museum key card. "Got it," he called.

At that moment, headlights swept across the room as a car drove up the long driveway. Ben peered out a window. It wasn't Abigail's car. As he and Riley watched, Abigail and a handsome man got out of the car. Ben recognized him immediately. It was Dr. Connor Hamilton, the White House curator.

"She's on a date," Ben said, his jaw clenching.

"Ben, you guys broke up. She's hot. It happens. Let's go," Riley said quickly. The last thing he wanted was to get caught breaking into Abigail's house—with her ex.

But it was too late. The key turned in the now unlocked door and Abigail walked in, a confused expression on her face. The confusion turned to annoyance when she saw Ben standing in the hall, holding a box. "What are you doing here?" she asked.

"I came back to pick up some final things," Ben told Abigail, his expression revealing nothing. Shifting his gaze, he greeted Connor.

"How'd you get in?" Abigail asked, annoyed by the turn the evening had taken. Then it hit her. She knew exactly how he had gotten in. "Riley! Come out here!" she shouted.

Sheepishly, Riley emerged from his hiding spot, one of the hall closets, and waved at Abigail. Aware that this was not the most comfortable of situations, Connor quickly said his good-byes. But not before confirming his next date with Abigail before he left. When the door closed behind him, Abigail glared at Ben.

"I can't believe that you broke in," she said. "What did you take?" She grabbed the box in Ben's hand—

only to find dish soap and shampoo. When she shot him a stern glare, he shrugged and handed over her key card, too.

"I need to see the page," Ben confessed.

"Why?" Abigail ranted. "Because you don't believe the seven document experts who authenticated it? You saw the page yourself. There is no treasure map on it."

Riley faced Ben. "I thought you said there was."

Ben shrugged. "It's not a treasure map per se. It's a cipher *leading* to a treasure." Then he turned to Abigail. "Did anyone spectral-image the page?"

Abigail shook her head. "No need to. All the ink writing on the page is clearly visible."

"Something could've been erased or could have faded," Ben pointed out.

Abigail was about to snap a response, but something stopped her. Ben was right. She couldn't argue that, but it made her no less angry.

"Come on, Abigail," he begged. "Just one peek with infrared." He watched her face and gave her a sly smile. "You can have the Boston Tea Tables."

"Both of them?" Abigail replied.

Ben had just made himself a deal.

CHAPTER FOUR

In the empty lab of the museum, Ben, Abigail, and Riley leaned over the Synchrotron, an X-ray machine. The room was dark save for the dull glow that came from the computer screen.

As Ben and Abigail stared at the ink writing illuminated on the screen, Riley started to shuffle his feet impatiently. They weren't finding anything.

"There are thousands of bands of infrared wavelengths. It takes time for the digital processing to bring out the latent images," Ben explained.

Riley shrugged. The screen still looked ominously blank to him. "Look at it this way," he said, trying to lighten the rather somber mood. "One hundred years from now, no one will remember anyone involved in the Lincoln assassination besides Booth."

"Do you know the origin of that expression, 'his name is mud'?" Ben retorted.

"Does anyone but you?" Riley countered.

"Dr. Samuel Mudd was convicted of being a coconspirator in the Lincoln assassination. The evidence was circumstantial, and he was later pardoned by Vice President Andrew Johnson, but it didn't really matter. Mudd's name is still infamous. I will not allow Thomas Gates's name to be mud."

As he spoke, Ben's eyes didn't leave the screen. He knew there had to be writing. Then, he saw something. "There!"

At first, all that Riley could make out were a few smudges. But slowly those smudges came clear, and the electrons of the machine did their work. Fragments of handwriting started to appear.

"It's a cipher," Ben said, excitement in his voice. "See how the letters are coupled? Playfair ciphers encode letters in pairs. It's exactly what Charles said was in the Booth diary. This proves his story!"

Abigail and Riley looked on as Ben's eyes raced over the screen. There were millions of words in the

English language, it could take forever to solve the cipher. Pushing aside any doubts, Ben asked for a printout.

Pressing a button, Abigail started the printer. When it was printed out, she handed the paper to Ben. Her fingers lingered in his as she looked into his eyes.

"Dr. Nichols is announcing the discovery of the page to the American Historical Consortium tomorrow," she said gently.

"Tomorrow?" Ben exclaimed. "Can't you ask him to wait until I can prove Thomas is innocent?"

Abigail stared at him. This stubbornness was exactly what had driven her away in the first place. And now, when he should have been doing everything in his power to act rationally, Ben was at it again. "What makes you so sure he is? What if you decipher the code and find out Thomas was involved in Lincoln's assassination?"

Ben looked her straight in the eye. "I refuse to believe that."

Abigail sighed. "You know," she said, "the man I once fell in love with cared about the truth, not just about being right."

"I am searching for the truth," Ben told her.

"Are you?" Abigail asked, before walking away.

Behind her, Ben watched her leave, his heart aching. What had become of them?

The next afternoon, at the FBI building, Agent Sadusky, the man who had unintentionally helped Ben on his quest to find the Templar Treasure, was hunched over a case file. His salt-and-pepper hair was neatly combed back, and his black suit was pressed perfectly.

"Looks like our old friend Gates is in the news again," Agent Hendricks said, entering the room and handing the older man the newspaper. The agent pointed to the article, "Missing Page of John Wilkes Booth Diary Discovered."

As Hendricks explained about Mitch Wilkinson and his part in bringing the page forward, Agent Sadusky's expression grew grave.

"What do we know about this Wilkinson?" the agent commanded.

"I don't know," Hendricks answered.

Sadusky shot the younger agent a stern look. The message was clear—he wanted information . . . now.

CHAPTER FIVE

Patrick Gates was seething. Staring at his computer screen, he watched as Dr. Nichols introduced Mitch Wilkinson. He was viewing the American Historical Consortium Web site, which was delivering the news of the Booth diary page—and Thomas Gates's now-terrible role in history.

Walking into his father's study, Ben took in the older man's handsome face. Patrick looked tired as he ran a hand through his gray hair, and Ben felt his heart clench. "Dad," he said gently, "will you stop watching that?"

Patrick looked over at his son. "It's on the Internet! There's no stopping it now." He paused.

"You know Nichols has pulled the Thomas Gates memorial," he said.

"I know," Ben said softly. "But do you want to beat this guy?" At his father's nod, Ben smiled. "Then let's prove that the Booth cipher leads to a treasure map. I've been thinking—Thomas must have broken the cipher. That's what got him killed." Ben knew that the Confederates would not have wanted their secret to fall into Union hands.

Tearing his gaze away from the computer screen, Patrick's expression grew thoughtful. His son was onto something. Thinking over the many times he had heard the story of Thomas, an expression popped into Patrick's head. "Grandpa said it was 'the debt that all men pay,'" the older man said.

Ben's eyes lit up and he looked over at his father. Thomas hadn't been using a random phrase—it was a clue! He had to call Riley!

A little while later, laptop in hand, Riley sat in Patrick's dining room, ready to crack a code. At Ben's urging, Riley typed in the word "death."

Noticing Riley's expression, Ben explained, "The debt all men pay is death."

Riley nodded as he punched the final letter into the program. L-A-B-O-U-L-_-_-E-L-A-D appeared on the screen.

"Nope. Gibberish," Riley said, disappointed.

But Ben and Patrick were far from disappointed.

"Laboulaye!" Ben cried.

"What is that?" Riley asked.

"It's a *who*," Ben said. "Édouard Laboulaye . . ." Grabbing the phone, Ben began to dial.

In another part of Washington, D.C., Abigail entered a modern restaurant and took in the stunning view. Beyond the large picture windows stood the Capitol, its white sides illuminated in the dark night. Glancing over at the bar, she saw her date for the evening— Mitch Wilkinson.

"Dr. Chase," Mitch said when she arrived at the bar. "Thank you for agreeing to meet me." With a nod, he indicated the empty bar stool next to him.

Gracefully, Abigail slipped onto it. When she was comfortable, she turned and met Mitch's eyes. "I was going to call you anyway about the diary page," she answered.

"Well, lucky for me, we share a common interest . . .

an excuse to get to know you better." Mitch flashed a smile, and Abigail found herself smiling back. "But yes, I am curious about the diary page."

Reaching into her purse, Abigail pulled out a multispectral photo. It was identical to the one Ben had made back in the lab and was now examining with his father. "We found some latent letter fragments," Abigail explained.

"Random letters. A cipher?" Mitch asked. "Has Dr. Gates seen this?"

At the mention of her ex's name, Abigail stiffened. "He's the one who made the discovery," she said bluntly.

Just then, Abigail's cell phone rang. Glancing at the caller ID, she looked up apologetically at Mitch. "I'm busy," she said into the phone.

"We cracked the cipher," Ben told her. "It's 'Laboulaye.' The cipher spells 'Laboulaye.'"

Abigail's interest was piqued, but she didn't show it. "So," she said.

"Why would Booth have a coded missive referencing a French mason, who wasn't KGC or even a Confederate?"

With another apologetic smile at Mitch, Abigail

stood up. Stepping away from the crowded bar, she gave her explanation to Ben. "Maybe the KGC was planning to kill Laboulaye, too. Laboulaye was a zealous advocate of Lincoln."

"Or," Ben hedged, "maybe there was a treasure map like Thomas Gates said there was, and Laboulaye had it."

Of course Ben would see it that way, Abigail thought. Anything to make sure his family's name remained untarnished. It didn't matter if his "facts" were circumstantial. Ben went on.

"We only got a partial on the next word. . . ." His voice trailed off as he stared at the laptop screen. "Laboulaye and then L-A-D. Lad? Ladder?"

"Lady!" Abigail shouted, a bit louder than she had meant to. Sheepishly looking back at the bar, Abigail noticed that Mitch was looking rather bored. "I have to go," she said quickly. With a definitive click, she hung up.

"Dr. Gates?" Mitch asked when Abigail was once again seated at the bar. When she answered yes, Mitch posed the next logical question. "I take it he cracked the cipher? I couldn't help but overhear. Laboulaye?"

Nodding, Abigail looked down at the bar counter. "That's what he thinks, at least."

This was an interesting twist. "Wasn't Laboulaye the one who first came up with the idea for the Statue of Liberty?" Mitch asked.

Back at Patrick's house, Ben looked down at the phone in his hand. "She hung up on me," he said, sounding rather shocked. Abigail knew what he was getting at. The Statue of Liberty! How could she have just hung up?

"Well, she took your call," Patrick said, trying to sound optimistic.

"You know," Riley pointed out, "there's a twenty-seven percent chance that permutations of incorrect cipher keys will result in legible phrases. This could be a false positive."

Ben shook his head. The cipher was right. He knew it and so did his father. "So the question is," Patrick said, jumping into the conversation, "which Statue of Liberty?"

"There's more than one?" Riley asked.

"There are three actually. One in New York, one in the Luxembourg Gardens, and the third on the River Seine in Paris."

As Riley stared at Ben in disbelief—where did he find out about this stuff?—Patrick smiled. He knew just where they needed to go. "But Laboulaye only referred to one as his 'lady.'"

Even though it was late in the evening, Agent Sadusky was at his desk. Agent Hendricks entered the office, with Agent Rachel Spellman close behind. They had figured the workaholic would be there.

"So," Hendricks said, "it turns out Mitch Wilkinson has two brothers, Seth and Daniel, who are both linked to a strip-mining operation in Uganda in 1997 and the looting of the Baghdad Museum in 2003." He handed the file to his boss.

Spellman elaborated. "Mitch Wilkinson ran a private security company which had contracts in Iraq during the invasion and in Uganda in the late nineties."

"These guys are trained mercenaries in addition to being black-market antiquities dealers," Hendricks said.

Agent Sadusky took a moment to review the file. Then he looked up at the two agents. "So, why does a black-market antiquities dealer give up a rare Civil War artifact, something he could have sold to a private collector for a good deal of money?"

CHAPTER SIX

Balancing his takeout dinner with one hand and fishing for his house keys with the other, Patrick Gates unlocked his front door. It was late, and he was ready to settle in for the night.

Suddenly, out of the shadows, a hand reached out and grabbed Patrick's arm. A moment later, a needle plunged into his skin and Patrick slipped into unconsciousness.

Stepping out of the shadows, Mitch Wilkinson, and his brothers, Seth and Daniel, quickly pulled Patrick into the house, but not before grabbing his cell phone and cloning it. Now whenever Patrick made or received a call, they'd be listening in.

When he came to, Patrick found himself blind-folded and tied up in what he guessed was one of his dining room chairs. What he did not know was that he was was also hooked up to a polygraph machine.

"What's going on?" Patrick asked, struggling to get free.

"Are you comfortable?" Mitch asked, finally speaking. When Patrick answered no, Mitch went on. "You're hooked up to a polygraph . . . so keep telling the truth, and this will be over soon."

"What do you want?" Patrick asked.

"Tell me about Édouard Laboulaye," Mitch said. "What did he know about the treasure map?"

Patrick was still. How did these men know about Laboulaye? He tried to be nonchalant as he replied, "I don't know."

The needles on the machine jumped. Mitch didn't have time for this. "I don't have to tell you that you're lying. Now, tell me. Why did the cipher say 'Laboulaye'?" When Patrick once again answered with a lie, Daniel pulled out a gun.

"Mr. Gates, please," Mitch said. "We're treasure hunters. Let's not kid ourselves about what we're capable of here. In treasure hunting, the end justifies the means."

"If I tell you, what's to stop you from killing me?" Patrick asked.

Mitch thought about that for a moment. "Your son commits crimes to a specific purpose, and I am no different. I will only kill you if you don't tell me."

"Statue of Liberty," Patrick finally said clearly. "Laboulaye hid the clue in the Statue of Liberty."

The three Wilkinson men all looked over at the machine. The needles didn't jump. Instead, the line was smooth and steady. Patrick was telling the truth.

"The Statue of Liberty wasn't built at the time that cipher was written," Mitch pointed out.

"The clue is in the torch," Patrick retorted. "Laboulaye was a poet. He wrote a poem entitled 'My Lady.'" The older Gates went on to explain that in the poem Laboulaye referred to a secret hidden in light.

Mitch smiled. They had gotten what they needed. Now they had to go see the large iron lady about a clue.

The next morning the three Wilkinson men were part of the crowds of tourists viewing the Statue of Liberty in Liberty Harbor, New York. Their eyes scanned the area, searching for some clue or reason the cipher led to this place. Making their way to an exhibit that displayed the statue's original torch, the men slowly circled it.

"There's nothing on it," Daniel said, frustrated.

As Daniel and Seth continued to pace, Mitch wandered over to another exhibit. Suddenly, he clenched his fists. "Maybe it's the wrong torch," he snapped. In front of him were replicas—of *three* statues.

They had been tricked.

At that moment, Ben Gates and Riley Poole were across the Atlantic in France with *another* group of tourists looking at *another* Statue of Liberty. While Ben was focused, Riley was jumpy, constantly looking over his shoulder. Ben had been lecturing about Thomas Gates and Confederate gold for months. People were bound to smell a treasure hunt. And Riley, for one, wasn't up for sharing the wealth or dealing with the more eccentric hunters. But when he mentioned would-be treasure seekers, Ben shrugged it off. He had bigger concerns.

"All those people think Thomas Gates conspired to assassinate Lincoln," he said.

Just then, Ben's cell phone rang, and Riley jumped. Looking at the screen, Ben saw it was his dad, and quickly picked up.

Hearing bits and pieces of the conversation between Ben and his dad, Riley grew even more worried. Treasure hunters had attacked Patrick, which meant they could be lurking around any corner. Little did Riley know they were actually listening in on the conversation through the cloned phone.

"So, I told them about the Statue of Liberty and the torch, but I didn't tell them which one," Patrick was saying.

"But they'll figure it out eventually," Ben answered. Suddenly something caught his eye. A bronze plaque with an inscription on it glinted in the sun. One word stood out—RESOLUTE.

He knew where they needed to go next. "Don't worry, Dad. We're going to Buckingham Palace."

Listening in, Mitch Wilkinson smiled. It looked like the treasure hunt was officially on.

CHAPTER SEVEN

In London, Ben and Riley quickly made their way to Buckingham Palace. Ben had gotten an appointment with the palace curator and was hoping to get some answers about the Resolute desk. After noticing the word on the plaque, Ben had quickly concluded that Resolute referred to the famous desk by that very name. Now, he just needed to see it.

While Riley waited for Ben in the reception area, he flipped through a tabloid newspaper, occasionally laughing at the more ridiculous stories. Suddenly, his eyes grew wide, and he flipped it closed just as Ben emerged from the curator's office.

"You understand," the curator was saying. "The

Resolute desk is in her Majesty's private wing. Not even *I'm* allowed in there."

"I understand," Ben said, gesturing to Riley to follow him outside. It was time for Plan B.

Once they were out in the main hall, Ben and Riley sat on a bench. Riley took out his laptop and began frantically typing. Within moments, he had managed to tap into the curator's computer. With a few more keystrokes, he pulled up the palace's schematics. Her Majesty's private wing was right next to the security center. They were going to need a disturbance.

Just as Riley voiced this concern, Ben's eyes widened. Following his friend's gaze, Riley saw Abigail walking toward the curator's office. Their disturbance had come to them!

A short while later, Abigail emerged from the curator's office. Ben and Riley were waiting.

"Ben, what are you doing?" she asked after a moment of stunned silence.

"You kick me out of my house, then follow me all the way here," Ben said by way of answering. "Doesn't that strike you as a bit, oh . . . inconsistent?"

Abigail was insulted. "I didn't follow you," she told them. They both looked at her incredulously. "You think I couldn't figure it out myself? Statue of Liberty? Twins stand 'resolute'?"

As their voices grew louder, the guard outside the curator's office took notice—which was *exactly* what Ben wanted. Ben continued to heckle Abigail until the guard finally pulled them aside. They were going to make a little visit—to the security center.

While Ben and Abigail were getting acquainted with security, Riley was taking a tour of the palace—but not for a history lesson. He followed his guide, nodding at the appropriate times, until he ducked into a men's room and set up his computer in a tiny stall. Within moments, he had tapped back into the system. Down in the security room, the lights on the main console that indicated whether doors were open or locked began to blink green, then red, then green. . . .

Just as the men in the security room took notice, Ben and Abigail's fake fight intensified. Luckily for their guard, the call came over his radio to come help with the breach. Apologizing to Ben and Abigail, he took off, leaving the bickering couple locked in the waiting area of the security center. As soon as they were alone, Ben rushed to the door. "Open up, Riley," he said into the small mic hidden in his clothes.

Inside the bathroom stall, Riley's fingers flew over the keys. With one last click, the security center's light flashed green. "You are cleared for takeoff," he said proudly.

Pushing the door open, Ben and Abigail slipped into the hallway and quickly made their way toward her Majesty's wing. Narrowly missing a guard, they ducked into the queen's study. In the corner of the room sat an antique writing desk.

Locking the door, they gazed at the historical desk in awe. While both of them had seen pieces of such value before, its historical significance still made the duo speechless. Ben just hoped they had been right and that the desk held an even greater treasure inside.

"What are we looking for?" Abigail whispered after a moment.

"Writing, a furniture maker's stamp, a pattern in the carvings," Ben whispered back. "It could be anything."

Nodding, Abigail moved closer and began to open and shut the drawers. She was just about to shut another one when Ben stopped her. At the bottom of the drawer was a stamp. "Look at this. 'Malcolm Gilvary, 1880'."

In the bathroom, Riley typed the name into the computer and informed Ben and Abigail that Gilvary made puzzle boxes.

With that piece of information, Ben reexamined the desk. Inset ball bearings made for glides along the bottom of the drawer. There were a series of notches as well. "I think these drawers work like the tumblers in a safe." He began to root around in all the drawers. "All we need is the combination. There are four drawers, so it'd be a series of four numbers."

Out in the hallway, a guard was talking on his handheld intercom. "Security door number seven reset," he said to the guard back at security central.

The guard at the desk looked at his monitor in confusion. All the doors in the wing were reading green, meaning open.

In his restroom stall, Riley watched the door monitors on his laptop. Ben and Abigail didn't have much time. The guards would soon catch on that something was happening with their security system.

Inside the study, Abigail made a suggestion. "It's a year!" she exclaimed.

"1492, 1776, or 1880, the year the desk was made," Ben suggested, growing more excited.

On the other end of the line, Riley got to work looking up everything from the queen's birth year to her coronation. . . .

Time was running out. The guards were coming down the hall, and Ben was still stumped by this numerical puzzle. He searched his brain for details that had led him to this point. "Try some HMS *Resolute* dates," Ben urged Riley, referencing the actual ship the wood had come from to make the desk. In the bathroom, Riley plugged in "Resolute" and spouted off a few more years. Still nothing.

"The Statue of Liberty's birthday," Ben said.

"Laboulaye's dinner!" exclaimed Abigail.

"1865," they said in unison.

Carefully, they pulled out the drawers to the corresponding notches, 1-8-6-5 . . . and there was a *thunk!* The top of the desk unlocked, and together Ben and Abigail lifted it open to reveal a hidden compartment. Inside was a dusty old piece of wood with enigmatic markings on it.

"These markings are pre-Columbian," Ben said, staring in disbelief.

Abigail was stunned, too. "But that would predate the Civil War by centuries."

Quickly, Ben and Abigail snapped photos. Abigail used her camera, and Ben shot with his cell phone.

"What do you think it says?" Abigail said to Ben.

Ben studied the markings. He hated to admit it, but he was stumped. "Well, I doubt it has anything to do with Confederate gold."

Back in the men's room stall, Riley was watching the palace's security system. All the unsecured lights that he had manipulated were now secure. He picked up his cell phone again.

"Guys," he said, "you really need to get back now."

Taking his own advice, Riley packed up his computer and scooted out of the restroom just as the guard who had escorted Ben and Abigail walked back into the now-empty security center waiting room.

CHAPTER EIGHT

Unbeknownst to Ben, Abigail, and Riley, they were not the only treasure seekers in the city of London. After listening in on Ben and Patrick's conversation, the Wilkinsons had found their way across the ocean. They were now among the many tourists visiting Buckingham Palace. But unlike the other tourists, they weren't looking at the famous building. They were looking for Ben and Riley. Mitch was on a tour inside the palace while Daniel and Seth surveyed the grounds. From an upstairs window, Mitch peered down to the quadrangle and spotted Riley. He took out his cell phone and called Daniel.

"I see one of them," Mitch said into the phone. "In the quadrangle."

Daniel looked around and spotted Riley. "Got him," he replied.

Ben and Abigail were rushing down a street to the meeting point they had arranged with Riley. They turned the corner—only to find Mitch standing there, a gun pointed at Riley's head!

"Wilkinson," Ben said flatly.

"Hello, Ben," Mitch said.

Just then, Daniel and Seth appeared behind Ben and Abigail—with guns!

"So now," Mitch coaxed, "why don't you just give us the camera?" He nodded at the obect in Abigail's hand.

Ben and Abigail looked over at Riley. Riley shrugged. Clearly, the armed Wilkinson men had persuaded Riley to tell them the truth about why they were at the palace.

Sighing, Abigail handed Daniel her camera. He viewed the digital camera screen, happy to see the photos recorded. Then he started to hand the camera to Mitch, knowing that he, too, would be pleased.

With lightning speed, Ben hit Daniel's hand with a swooping upswing and sent the camera flying into the air. As Daniel looked up at the camera, Ben plunged his elbow into Daniel's stomach. Daniel doubled over and Ben kneed him in the face, sending him down to the ground.

Riley took his cue from Ben and shoved Mitch, knocking him backward. Regaining his balance, Mitch aimed his gun at Riley, ready to shoot, but Ben's foot kicked the gun free.

Abigail and Seth, meanwhile, were also looking up at the flying camera, which gave Ben the opening to punch Seth in the stomach and Abigail clearance to catch the camera. Ben, Riley, and Abigail tore off down a crowded street. They dodged in and out of pedestrians and then spotted their BMW rental car.

"I'm driving!" Riley called, racing Ben to the left side of the car.

Ben calmly got into the right side. Riley had forgotten—in London, drivers sat on the opposite side. As Abigail climbed into the backseat, Ben started up the car.

The Wilkinsons quickly recovered and chased after the threesome. Seeing them get into the car, they immediately showered it with gunfire and the back window shattered.

"Are you all right?" Ben called back to Abigail.

"I'm fine," she answered. "What about you?"

Their eyes met in the rearview mirror.

"I'm good," Ben said with a smile.

Up in the front seat, Riley brushed the glass shards out of his hair. "I'm a little cold," he said. "Thanks for asking."

The Wilkinsons were not ready to give up the chase. The raced down the street, looking for a car. Mitch darted in front of a Mercedes. Behind the wheel, the young driver's eyes grew wide. Seth and Daniel opened the doors and climbed in the car.

"Hey!" the driver yelled. "This is my dad's car!"

Mitch didn't care. He dragged the young man out of the car and jumped into the driver's seat. Flooring the gas pedal, he sped off, his eyes never leaving Ben's car, which was up ahead.

The streets were congested with traffic, but that didn't stop Ben. He weaved in and out of lanes like he was playing a video game.

"Can't you go any faster?" Abigail demanded from the backseat.

"Maybe if there was one less passenger," Ben sang out. Then he downshifted and swerved around a large truck.

Meanwhile, Mitch was gaining on the BMW, and soon got close enough for Daniel to power down his window for a clean shot. Ben, Abigail, and Riley all ducked as more bullets sprayed the car. Whipping the wheel around, Ben stepped harder on the gas and peeled away from the Wilkinsons, fishtailing onto a bridge that crossed the Thames River. Mitch overshot the turnoff but quickly brought the car around and continued the pursuit, which was now headed straight toward the Waterloo train station.

Ben had little choice. He couldn't risk the chase going where so many people would be in the way. He cut the wheel sharply to the left, leaving the road and crashing down an embankment. The car barreled down the hill before smashing through a barbed-wire fence that surrounded the train yard. The train yard was a wide area with a series of railroad tracks that led in and out of the Eurostar tunnels.

Abigail looked over her shoulder. She watched as Mitch maneuvered his car over the embankment in hot pursuit. "They're not stopping," Abigail reported.

Not missing a beat, Ben replied. "Neither are we!"

He drove on, headed straight toward one of the tunnel openings.

"Ben," Riley called out, "those are train tunnels."

"I have an idea," Ben said, his hands clutching the steering wheel. He drove the car onto a set of tracks.

"There are trains in there!" Riley exclaimed. "Fast ones!"

"Not in the service tunnel," Ben replied and drove straight into the entrance.

But Mitch was not giving up, and he steered his car into the tunnel entrance as well. The two cars tore down the tunnel as if they were speeding trains.

Riley was not happy, especially when he noted a sign announcing exactly *what* tunnel they had just entered. "Um," he said, trying to get Ben's attention, "this tunnel's twenty-five miles long!"

Checking back on the Wilkinson car, Abigail saw the Mercedes gaining on them. They needed to do something—fast.

"Hold on!" Ben yelled. He spun the wheel and hit the brakes. The car turned, blocking the tunnel. "Get out!" he screamed. "Get out!"

Abigail and Riley scrambled out of the car and

followed Ben toward a door with a sign that read, CHUNNEL ACCESS PASSAGEWAY.

Behind them, Mitch slammed on the brakes, and his car skidded to a stop. The Wilkinsons all jumped out of the car, and began to chase Ben, Abigail, and Riley.

Ben reached the door first and punched a button to open it. The access door swung open just as an oncoming train whooshed by at top speed. The three-some sprinted down a short passageway just as Mitch appeared in the doorway behind them. He raised his gun and fired a few rounds.

"Down!" Ben commanded.

Abigail, Riley, and Ben dove, and tumbled down a few dark steps. Abigail landed hard, and the camera she had been clutching in her hand flew from her grasp.

"Ben!" she cried out. "The camera! I dropped it!"

Bullets began to fly, hitting the walls around Ben, Abigail, and Riley. There was no time to go back.

"Get to the other side!" Ben yelled.

Ben grabbed Abigail's hand, and the three of them lunged across the tracks just as another train blasted by them with a thunderous roar.

The Wilkinsons emerged on the other side of the tracks just as the train flew by. By the time the endless stream of passenger cars passed, Ben, Abigail, and Riley were nowhere in sight. Mitch sighed heavily. He never liked to lose. But then he looked down and a smile spread across his face. There, at his feet, was Abigail's camera.

Ben and his friends might have escaped, but Mitch had the camera and that was of far greater value.

CHAPTER NINE

Back in Washington, a knock at the door sent Patrick Gates rushing for his baseball bat. Holding it tightly in his hands, he made his way to the front door. Before he could turn the knob, the door burst open, revealing Ben and Riley.

"Welcome home," Patrick called, breathing a big sigh of relief. "Can't wait to see what you got!"

Before Ben could answer, Abigail appeared. Seeing her familiar—but long absent—face, Patrick smiled.

"Abigail!" he cried. "What a pleasant surprise!"

"Hello, Patrick," she said sweetly. Reaching over, she gave him a kiss on the cheek.

Patrick couldn't contain his excitement. "How

Thomas Gates and his son, Charles, are so involved
in their maps that they don't even realize the
Civil War has ended!

John Wilkes Booth has one task to complete—
assassinate President Lincoln.

Benjamin Franklin Gates is determined to clear his
family's name . . . and find the treasure.

Riley Poole's book signing is not as well-attended
as he had hoped.

Ben calls his ex-girlfriend, Abigail Chase, to tell
her that he's discovered a clue!

Mitch Wilkinson will stop at nothing to get his
hands on the treasure.

Patrick Gates believes his ancestors were heroes—
not villians.

Abigail has had enough of Ben's conspiracy
theories and obsession with treasure.

Ben brings Abigail to see his mother, Emily, who he
hopes will be able to translate one of the clues.

Ben asks FBI Agent Sadusky for information
on the *Book of Secrets*.

At the president's birthday party, Ben shows
him a special map.

Riley and Abigail race through the Library
of Congress.

Patrick and Emily set aside their differences to
help Ben decipher the clues.

Ben, Riley, and Abigail will have to work with
Mitch to get the treasure.

nice to see you two together again," he said as he watched Ben and Abigail.

"Oh, well . . ." Abigail began.

Ben finished her sentence for her. "We're not," he said.

"Oh," Patrick said, uncomfortably. Quickly, he changed the topic to the issue at hand. "So what did you find?"

Moments later, the group was huddled around Riley's open laptop. The photo of the plank from the desk flashed on the screen. Mitch and his family may have thought they were the only ones with a lead, but they were wrong. Ben had e-mailed the photo from his camera phone to Riley's account. Now they just had to solve the next clue faster than the Wilkinsons.

Patrick's eyes locked on the glyphs spread across the plank. "After all my years with you-know-who, I can tell you these are definitely precolonial Native American markings.

"Easily over five hundred years old," Ben said in a hushed whisper. "Do you think it's Olmec?"

"I don't know, but I can identify this symbol," Patrick said, pointing to the screen. "Cíbola."

"The City of Gold," Ben said, amazement in his voice. What had they uncovered this time?

In Patrick's study, Ben took a book down from one of his father's cluttered shelves. He flipped open the volume and showed the page to Riley. "In 1527, a Spanish ship wrecked on the Florida coast. There were only four survivors. One was a slave by the name of Esteban, who saved a local tribe's dying chief with his knowledge of herbs and medicines." Ben pointed to an ink drawing of the sixteenth-century shipwreck. "As a reward, he was taken to their sacred city, a city built from solid gold." Ben turned the page and showed a drawing of Esteban kneeling before the City of Gold. In faint writing were the words, *Esteban Mira Cíbola, 1533*.

Riley and Abigail stared at the drawing, hanging on every word of the story.

"Later, when Esteban tried to find the city again," Ben continued, "he never could."

"Probably because he didn't have a cell phone picture of the map," Riley quipped.

Ben ignored Riley and looked over at his father. "I'm going to go talk to her."

Riley glanced at Abigail to see if she knew who Ben was referring to. "His mom," Abigail whispered.

Patrick's eyes narrowed. "There's a reason we

haven't spoken in thirty-two years. We have nothing in common."

"Me!" Ben shouted. He needed his dad to support this next move. Ben's mom was one of the country's leading experts on early-American languages. It was vital they talked to her.

Patrick's expression softened. His son had a point. He would go, but he was positive nothing good could come out of a meeting with Dr. Emily Appleton. Nothing.

A while later, the four stood in front of a large brick building. All around them, University of Maryland students made their way to and from classes. While Ben was unbothered by the scene, Patrick was visibly nervous.

"Dad, will you relax?" Ben pleaded. "It'll be fine."

"You're right," Patrick said, trying to compose himself. "Maybe she's lost her memory—and she won't recognize me."

With that reassuring thought, the group walked into the building and down the corridor lined with professors' offices. At the one marked Dr. Appleton, they paused. Suddenly the door flew open, and a grumbling student pushed past. Behind her was Emily. She was sitting at her desk, working on some papers in front of her and didn't even look up. Beautiful as well as brainy, she was clearly a force to be reckoned with.

"No, I don't grade on a curve," she said, still looking at her papers. "No one got higher than a C minus. And no, there will be no makeup."

"Hi, Mom," Ben said.

At the sound of her son's voice, Emily looked up and her face softened. "Benjamin! Abigail!" she cried. "What a nice surprise!" Then her eyes fell on Patrick. "Oh," she sighed.

"See?" Patrick said to Ben. "One syllable, a knife to the heart. She can do that."

"I can also locate my toothbrush," she told Patrick. Though many years had passed, Emily was quick to jump back into an argument they had clearly been waging for quite some time.

"I wasn't the one who left our toothbrushes in Marrakesh. I stowed them both in the travel case, as instructed. . . ."

"And who was in charge of arranging the taxi?" Emily asked, interrupting him.

As the pair continued to volley insults back and forth, Abigail looked on in awe. "Those two really haven't seen each other in thirty-two years?" Abigail asked, amazed that their longstanding argument could be taken up so quickly. Well, not as amazed as she'd care to admit.

"Uh, Mom," Ben interrupted, "I need you to look at this." Holding up the photo of the plank, he watched as recognition filled Emily's face. "We think it might be Olmec," he finally said.

Moving closer, Emily studied the photo. "Definitely proto-Zoquean," she exclaimed.

"We were hoping you could translate it," Patrick said a bit sheepishly, from his spot on the couch.

"Does it involve another treasure?" Emily asked, her face tightening.

"Mom, please," Ben begged. "It's important."

"All right," she said, picking up the photo. "This glyph here means 'tall' or 'towering.' And this means 'stand.' Stand at the highest point."

Ben took a piece of paper off his mother's desk and began to write.

"Find the noble bird which sits on the warrior fallen in tears," she continued. "He will take your hand and give you passage . . ." Her voice trailed off as she realized what she was reading. "I know what you think this is. A treasure map to Cíbola!"

"That's exactly what it is," Patrick protested.

"Dad," Ben pleaded, trying to get him to focus and not pick a fight.

"This glyph means 'axis mundi,' the center of the world," Emily retorted. "Treasure is *your* axis mundi."

Desperately, Ben tried to get his mother back to the translation, but the banter between her and his father continued.

"You used to like that," Patrick said. "You fell in love with me on a treasure hunt."

Emily waved her hand in the air dismissively. "That wasn't love. That was excitement, adrenaline, and . . . tequila."

"Well," Patrick said with a sly smile. "The treasure hunting paid off, in case you haven't read the papers lately."

"*Ben* found the treasure," Emily spat. "*You've* done nothing!"

Ben shook his head. He had suddenly realized how self-absorbed his parents had been throughout his childhood. "I thought that you were cool because you'd leave me alone to do my own thing," he said. "But you were just both all wrapped up in yourselves."

Ben's words hit Patrick and Emily hard, and they both looked at him, guilt written all over their faces.

Tearing off Ben's notes from the pad, Abigail broke the uncomfortable silence in the office. "What else does this say?" she asked Emily.

"That's all," Emily told them. "These glyphs here," she said, pointing back to the image. "They're only partials." Then she looked right at Patrick. "Sorry. Looks like you've got only half a treasure map here." She looked away and smirked. "I'm not surprised."

With no more to learn from Emily, they left her office and walked across the quad. "We have to get the rest of the map," Ben said after a few moments of pained silence. Abigail and Riley agreed.

"You know where it is?" Patrick asked, still reeling from the heated exchange with Emily.

"Well, the inscription on the Paris statue said, 'these twins stand resolute,'" Ben quoted.

"The map must have been divided between the two Resolute desks," Abigail finished.

Patrick stopped walking and faced the pair. "Wait," he said, question in his eyes.

Ben nodded his head. "Unfortunately, yes."

"That's the president's desk," Patrick said.

Riley turned, stunned. "The president . . . our president?"

Ben nodded again.

Riley thought out loud. "But that . . . so the . . ." His mind was spinning with logistics. "The White House?"

"The Oval Office, to be exact," Ben said.

Riley's mouth dropped open. Buckingham Palace was one thing, but the White House? How were they going to pull that off?

CHAPTER TEN

Dr. Nichols's office in the museum reflected his long career as a curator, as well as his many interests. The room was packed with history books, memorabilia from the Civil War, and a large collection of Masonic items. Dr. Nichols was a collector and a scholar.

Mitch Wilkinson was banking on that knowledge and experience. It was why the Wilkinsons went to him in the first place. Nichols also had friends in high places—who possessed important documents.

"You murdered a judge," Dr. Nichols said now, turning to look at the three Wilkinson men sitting in his office.

"Well," Mitch responded, "pardon my saying, Dr. Nichols, but good manners only get you so far." He gave a knowing look to Daniel and Seth. "Now," he went on, "will you please try to focus on the task at hand?"

Dr. Nichols walked over to the table in front of the couch. On top were the photos Abigail had taken of the queen's desk. He considered the markings on the plank. "It looks pre-Columbian. Very early," he commented.

"Can you translate it?" Daniel asked.

"Are you kidding?" Dr. Nichols said. "This is an extinct language. There's only a handful of people who study languages like these."

Not being swayed from the task at hand, Seth called out, "And where are we to find them?"

Dr. Nichols sighed. "Universities, I suppose. But you don't even have the whole thing." He pointed to the photographs. "These glyphs here, they're cut off."

"So how are we supposed to find the rest of the map?" whined Seth.

Mitch smiled. "We won't have to. Gates will."

"Maybe this was a mistake," Dr. Nichols said to the three men, his thoughts returning to the news Mitch had given him upon first arriving. "What if they trace the murder back to me?" He was growing more and more nervous. "Judge Turman was a thirty-third degree Master Mason. *I'm* a Mason."

Mitch regarded Dr. Nichols. "Well, I'm not going to tell anyone you told me that he had the Booth diary page," he said. "Are *you* going to tell anyone?"

"Of course, I'm not!" cried Dr. Nichols.

"Good," Mitch told him. "Because the Masons will never admit to ever having had that page."

This still didn't make Dr. Nichols feel better. "I don't think I have the stomach for this anymore." He looked Mitch in the eyes. "I don't want anything. You can have my share. I just want out."

The Wilkinsons all stifled a laugh. It was too late for that. Dr. Nichols had been instrumental in getting their plan in motion. But that by no means made him indispensable.

Mitch put his hand on Dr. Nichols's shoulder. "Very generous of you," he said, knowing that he would have to do away with Dr. Nichols—just as he had the judge.

CHAPTER ELEVEN

The White House lawn was jam-packed with people participating in the annual Easter Egg Roll. The green expanse had been converted into a carnival, with tons of activities for kids of all ages, such as face painting, egg-dyeing, egg-roll races, and, of course, meeting the Easter Bunny.

Walking amongst the festivalgoers, Ben and Abigail found themselves having a good time. It was hard to remember that their agenda for being there was far different from that of all the other guests.

At the ring-toss booth, Ben expertly threw a ring onto a soda bottle and won a stuffed bunny. "You have quite an aptitude for childish pursuits,"

Abigail noted, a smile tugging at her mouth.

Before he could retort, a boy pulled on Ben's jacket. "I know you!" he said. "Your great-great-grandfather killed President Lincoln!" he shouted.

Ben's face grew red. "No," he calmly explained. "That would be John Wilkes Booth."

"Eisenschiml says that Booth was just a tool in a greater conspiracy that involved men in Lincoln's own cabinet," the boy stated.

"Eisenschiml's book is filled with spotty research and false assumptions," Ben said, his jaw clenched.

"How do you explain why Lincoln's bodyguard left his post that night?" the boy said, firing his question at Ben more like a seasoned debater than a child.

"President Lincoln had never been accompanied by guards when attending the theater, especially on Good Friday," Ben replied, his patience wearing thin.

The boy kept up his questioning. "How do you explain why all bridges out of Washington were closed except one . . . the one Booth needed to escape?"

"How old are you?" Ben asked.

"Eight and a half," the boy replied.

"Why don't you come back in nine and a half years, and we'll discuss this then?" Ben told him.

The boy pointed to the bunny in Ben's hand that he had just won from the ring-toss game. "Can I have your bunny?

"No," Ben said.

The boy made a face and ran off. As Ben tucked the bunny into his pocket, another voice came across the lawn.

"Abby!" Connor called out. He ran up to Abigail. "So glad you decided to come." Then Connor saw Ben standing next to her. "And Gates," he added, visibly agitated that Abigail was there with her ex.

When she and Ben had come up with their plan for getting into the Oval Office, Abigail knew that the situation might get a bit strained. Putting Ben in the same vicinity with one of her suitors was just inviting trouble. "We just ran into each other," she said now, hoping to sound nonchalant.

Anxious to move the plan along, Ben egged Abigail on. "So, are you going to ask him?"

Connor beamed at Abigail. He was quite smitten with her and clearly poised to do anything for her. "Ask me what?"

Abigail smiled coyly, "I wouldn't want to impose."

Ben couldn't help himself. "What she means is,

she doesn't think you can," he told Connor.

Connor took the bait. "Doesn't think I can what?" he asked.

"She wants to see the Oval Office," Ben told him.

"I know," Abigail said. "It's too much to ask."

"No," Connor said quickly. "I can do that."

Abigail smiled. A few moments later, the three-some walked into the famous oval room. Ben and Abigail's eyes immediately went to the Resolute desk—a twin to the one back at Buckingham Palace. Connor noted Abigail looking at the famous desk, and he started to spout his knowledge about the history of it, hoping to impress her.

Struggling not to roll his eyes, Ben interrupted the other man. "Abby," he said, deliberately using the nickname that Connor seemed so fond of calling her, "did you lose an earring?"

Abigail, catching on quickly, put her hand to her ear. She deftly slipped off her earring. Then, with tears in her eyes, she said, "These earrings were given to me by my grandmother."

"I suppose we'd better look for it," Ben said. "We wouldn't want anyone finding an earring that doesn't belong to the First Lady in the Oval Office."

Connor agreed wholeheartedly. "Excellent point."

Abigail fell to her hands and knees and began to search for the "missing" earring. Connor followed.

"We should retrace your steps," Ben said. "I'll check over here." Ben made his way to the Resolute desk as Abigail steered Connor over to the fireplace on the opposite side of the room. As Ben quietly started to pull out desk drawers, he noticed that the inquisitive boy from the Easter Egg Roll was standing in the window. Ben quickly gestured for him to move away, but the headstrong boy shook his head no. Thinking fast, Ben pulled the stuffed bunny from his pocket and held it up as a bribe. The boy nodded, and the deal was struck—the boy wouldn't say a word, and Ben would give him the bunny.

With that taken care of, Ben continued to search the desk. Finally, with a click, a drawer opened to reveal another secret compartment. Unfortunately, the muffled clunk of the drawer caught Connor's attention. He looked up from under the couch where he had been searching. Desperate to keep him occupied, Abigail adeptly dropped her earring next to Connor's hand. Then she started to gush.

"Connor!" she cried. "You found it!"

"I did?" Connor asked.

Abigail gave Connor a big hug, making sure he was not facing the desk where Ben was staring, his eyes wide. There was no plank revealing glyphs. Instead, the presidential seal stared up at him. Shaking his head, Ben snapped a photo.

Across the room, Connor pulled out of the hug, and Abigail panicked. Ben wasn't finished yet. So she grabbed Connor and kissed him! Ben looked up and cleared his throat. Abigail broke off the kiss, leaving Connor a little dazed—and Ben a little jealous.

A short while later, Ben and Abigail joined Patrick and Riley in Lafayette Park to share what they had learned about the Oval Office Resolute desk.

"The brightest men in our country have sat at that desk for over one hundred years," Patrick said. "Of course one of them found the map."

"There was a symbol stamped onto the felt," Ben said, displaying the presidential seal he had snapped with his digital camera.

"That's not the seal," Abigail said as she studied the picture of the eagle. "It's holding a scroll instead of olive branches."

Riley grabbed the camera, and gave Ben, Patrick, and Abigail a stern look. "You guys," he said, "I sent you all a copy of my book. Did *none* of you read it?" Riley noticed their sheepish, guilty looks. They really hadn't read it! Crossing his arms, he stared them down. "I'm not going to *tell* you. You can read about it . . . IN MY BOOK." And with that he turned and walked away. Ben, Abigail, and Patrick followed.

A few moments later, the four stood at the trunk of Ben's car and watched as he rummaged through various moving boxes. Finally, his hand closed around a small, wrapped package. Pulling off the paper, he revealed Riley's book—still in pristine condition.

"Chapter thirteen," Riley said.

Opening to the appropriate page, Ben's eyes widened. "The President's Secret Book," he scoffed at the chapter heading. With a groan, he tossed the book back in his trunk.

Riley was not dissuaded. "Don't tell me you've never heard of the president's secret book?" he said. "The book filled with stuff only the president gets to know? Like who really killed JFK and what's really going on in Area 51."

Before he could go on, Abigail interrupted.

"That's an urban legend. No one's ever seen it."

"Except for every president of the United States," Riley retorted. Picking the book back up, he flipped to another page and pointed to a photo marked "Roswell." In the corner was the same symbol Ben had seen in the Resolute desk. Riley again flipped the pages, this time stopping on a page marked "Marilyn Monroe, Autopsy." Again, the seal could be seen stamped onto the paperwork. "The eagle and scroll," Riley said. "That means whatever was in those memos has been put into the president's book."

For a moment, no one spoke. Then Patrick looked over at Riley. "You think whatever was on that plank . . . is now *in* the president's book?"

"How do we prove it?" Abigail asked.

"How do we find it?" Riley added.

Ben took the camera back. "I know a man who knows all about presidents . . . and symbols."

CHAPTER TWELVE

Agent Sadusky sat at his office desk, holding Ben's digital camera in his hands. He stared at the image on the screen before looking over at Ben. Silently, he slid the camera back to him.

"I suggest you not show this to anyone else," the agent said softly.

"Then, you know what the symbol means?" Ben asked. "Does the president have a secret book or not?"

"Now why would I know that?" Sadusky replied, trying not to smile.

"Because of the forty-three men who have ever been president of the United States of America, fifteen of them are confirmed Freemasons," Ben explained. "You're a thirty-third degree Master Mason. If anyone knows if that book exists, it's you."

"You like ducks?" was all Sadusky said.

A few moments later, the two men stood at the edge of a duck pond. In his hand, Sadusky held a loaf of bread. Ben held Riley's book.

"There is a book," the agent told Ben as they walked along a tree-lined pond.

"Why tell me out here?" Ben asked.

"In my office," Sadusky gestured in the direction of the FBI building, "I'm a federal agent. Out here, I'm speaking to you as a Mason."

After a pause, Sadusky's face softened. "Do you know who Judge Gregory Turman is?"

Ben shook his head no.

"He died three weeks ago," the agent said. "He was the highest thirty-third degree Master Mason in the order.

"Friend of yours?"

"He was the custodian, for a time, of an artifact of some significance—the Booth diary page," Sadusky confessed.

"Wilkinson *stole* it?" Ben asked in astonishment.

"I can't prove it. There's no evidence that Judge Turman ever had the page in his possession."

They continued to look at the water, and Ben pressed on. "Why would the Masons hold on to the page?"

"Because, like you, they believe it might contain information that was intended for them."

"The missive the KGC intercepted in 1865 was intended for a Mason?" Ben asked. That would mean that Ben was right—that his ancestor had only been trying to help keep Mason information *away* from the KGC. That he had nothing to do with Lincoln's assassination.

Sadusky paused as if unsure whether to go on. "Not *a* Mason. *The* Mason. Confederate General Albert Pike."

Ben's eyes grew wide. This mystery went much deeper than he could ever have imagined. "I need to see the president's book. Where is it kept?"

"Only the current president knows," Sadusky said. "The book is passed from president to president, and each one changes its hiding place."

Ben turned to face the agent. "Can you get it for me?"

"I would like to see that book as much as you

would," he said. Then he sighed. "I'm sorry. The only way you're ever going to see that book is if you get elected president."

After leaving Sadusky at the FBI building, Ben made his way back to his father's house. He quickly filled Abigail, Riley, and his father in on his conversation with the agent.

"Even if you were married to the president, he'd never admit the book exists," Riley said when Ben had finished. "Let alone tell you what's in it."

"If I can just get him alone—" Ben sighed.

Riley raised an eyebrow. "How're *you* going to get him alone?"

Ben was silent as he thought about Riley's question. It *was* a daunting risk, but not *totally* impossible. "Thomas gave his life for the Union," he said. "Which is why we cannot have him remembered as a conspirator in the assassination of a man who brought this nation together."

Slamming his hand down on the table, he looked at the others. "So, how am I going to get him alone?" he asked. "I'm gonna kidnap the president of the United States."

CHAPTER THIRTEEN

Inside the White House press secretary's office, a roomful of aides were busy talking on phones and typing at computers. The president's birthday was rapidly approaching, and plans for his party were being finalized by the minute. The press secretary was juggling a few tasks at once in his typical harried state, and he was in no mood to deal with any unnecessary complications. Unfortunately, a rather large one was about to present itself—courtesy of a few well-timed calls from Ben and his friends.

Hesitantly approaching the press secretary's side, one of the aides cleared his throat. The secretary shot the aide a glare as if to say, "get on with it." The aide spoke up. "Some historian is claiming the Spencer Landmark Hotel was used for regular Klan meetings in the late 1800s," he said quickly.

"Do we know if that's true?" the press secretary asked warily. That was where the president's party was supposed to take place.

But then another aide called over to him. "I've got *The Washington Gazette*. They want a quote on. . . ." Then the aide read, "'Is the president trying to make a statement by holding his birthday party at a hotel affiliated with the Ku Klux Klan?'"

"Get my list of approved alternatives!" the press secretary yelled.

Immediately, all the aides in the room began to call the alternative sites—but thanks to Ben and friends, they were all booked. Except for one . . . Mount Vernon.

Mount Vernon, the grand estate that had once belonged to the first president of the United States, George Washington, was a picturesque mix of beautifully landscaped lawns and well-maintained buildings. On this particular evening, Mount Vernon was decked out with tents, lights, and flowers to celebrate the current president's birthday. The attendees were all dressed in their finest black-tie clothing, and limousines lined the expansive driveway. It looked like a scene out of a modern-day fairy tale—plus a few Secret Service agents.

On the Potomac, the river that bordered one side of the estate, Ben and Patrick were in a rowboat looking a little less formal. They could make out the lights from the party up the shoreline. Ben slipped on a snorkel face mask and fastened the zipper on the wet suit he was wearing.

"Whatever happened to you and Abigail?" Patrick whispered, looking around nervously.

"Not a good time, Dad," Ben replied, nodding at their surroundings.

"All relationships go through ups and downs," Patrick said wisely. "You gotta learn to stay the course."

Ben sighed. He loved his father, but now was not the time for a heart-to-heart. And, he noted, it was rather ironic that his very single father was giving *him* relationship advice. "Maybe the Gates men just weren't meant to live with other people," he said, putting an end to the conversation.

He grabbed a backpack off the boat's floor and got ready to dive in.

"Wait!" Patrick called. "Don't forget the gift." He handed Ben a present sealed in a waterproof bag, and Ben slipped it into his backpack.

Diving into the cool water, Ben used his flashlight to see through the murky river. Without too much effort, he made his way to an old pier and lifted himself out of the water. Opening his backpack, he pulled a tuxedo out of a waterproof bag and slipped it on. "Just once," he muttered to himself, "I'd like to wear this thing to a party I was actually invited to."

He grabbed his gift and put it in his tux jacket. Then he pulled out a bottle of champagne and two glasses before quickly stowing the bag in some bushes. Noticing two Secret Service agents up ahead, he started to stagger and sway as though he had been drinking for hours.

"Hey!" Ben called out. "You guys didn't happen to see a cute brunette wandering around here, did you?" When the agents shook their heads no, Ben thanked them, and then, ever so nonchalantly, headed toward the tents.

He was in.

CHAPTER FOURTEEN

Ben walked onto the manicured back lawn, where a string quartet was playing and teams of Secret Service agents were milling about. He passed a group of men and nodded hello. "Good evening, senators," he said. Weaving in and out of groups, Ben kept his eyes on the president. He was standing in a circle with a collection of noted movers and shakers.

"Remember, and spread the word," the president said to the group with a smile. "Campaign-contribution limits are not enforced on the president's birthday."

The group of men laughed, and the president broke out of the circle to continue making his rounds. Ben stepped up.

"Happy birthday, Mr. President," Ben said. When

he saw the president looking at him blankly, he added, "Ben Gates. The Templar Treasure?"

The name clicked, and the president shook his hand firmly. "Right, Ben Gates. My Lindbergh Award winner."

"I can't tell you what a thrill it is to be invited here," Ben told him.

The president grinned. "You probably have the Secret Service hopping right now, considering your newly discovered lineage."

Ben chuckled at the president's joke, trying to appear to be good-natured about the comment. But he couldn't help notice that the Secret Service agents *were* keeping a close eye on him.

Taking the gift out of his pocket, Ben leaned in to the president. "I know you're a great admirer of George Washington."

Out of the corner of his eye, Ben watched the agents. He knew that his time was running out. The president unwrapped the gift and was immediately pleased to see the hand-drawn map of Mount Vernon signed by George Washington, and clearly dated 1778.

"It belonged to my great uncle. He got it from the

granddaughter of a slave named Charlotte, who once worked here at Mount Vernon," Ben explained. Then he pointed to a spot on the grounds. "We're standing right here," Ben continued, "and right over here is an underground tunnel. An escape route for Washington's family . . ."

The president turned to face Ben, his eyes sparkling. "Do you think it's still there?"

"There's only one way to find out," Ben said. Together the two men turned and walked across the lawn, Secret Service close behind.

Moments later, Ben and the president found themselves in the Mount Vernon stables, looking at an open door that led to a cellar. Suddenly, an agent walked out and nodded to his boss. "All clear, sir."

Once safely down the cellar stairs, the president unfolded the map. "According to this," he told Ben, "it should be here somewhere. . . ."

"Over here . . ." Ben said, nodding at an iron Washington family coat of arms. Reaching out, Ben rubbed his hands on the ironwork, looking for a lever or hitch. Curious, the president put his hand on the fixture as well. With a loud groan, a section of wall in the cellar moved, revealing . . . a tunnel! They had found the secret passage! Within moments, the two men disappeared inside as the wall slid closed behind them.

At the top of the stairs, the agent heard an odd sound and bolted down the steps. To his amazement, the brick room was empty.

"We have a breach in zone nine!" he cried into his mic.

"Repeat?" the other agent asked, pushing hard on his earpiece.

Lifting his wrist to his mouth, Craig repeated his report. "Falcon has left the nest. Repeat, Falcon is in the open."

But the Falcon was not quite in the open. He was, at that very moment, in Washington's secret tunnel watching as the sliding wall closed, effectively concealing them in the cellar.

Ben turned to the president. "I'm sorry, Mr. President," he said with great sincerity. "I need to ask you a question that I know you couldn't answer unless we were alone."

"I'm not answering *any* question, and you are going to prison," the president stated. "How soon you open that door will determine for how many years. Right now, you're looking at five to ten."

Ignoring the president's statement, Ben forged on. "Sometime between 1880 when the Resolute desk was placed in the Oval Office and now, one of our presidents found a secret compartment in it."

"You realize," the president said, "you are now number one on the Secret Service, NSA, CIA, and the FBI Most Wanted lists."

Ben went on to explain about finding the Resolute desks in Buckingham Palace and in the Oval Office. And then, how the plank that led to the City of Gold in the presidential desk had been taken away, replaced by the presidential seal.

The president did not seem affected by this piece of news, but Ben went on speaking. "I believe the whereabouts of that plank is now hidden in the president's book, the book known only to the presidents. It contains all of our nation's secrets."

The president scoffed at this remark. "That's the most ridiculous thing I've ever heard."

In the cellar, agents were checking all the walls of the brick room.

The lead agent was getting more anxious. "I want a crowbar! I want a jackhammer! I want a bulldozer! And I want them now!"

All the agents in the room scattered to follow orders. Then the lead agent raised his wrist and spoke into his mic. "Alert the vice president," he said.

The president, meanwhile, was gazing down a long tunnel with side tunnels branching off in all directions.

"I saw the seal in the desk," Ben said softly, not giving up. "The map was there."

The president stared at Ben. "And you won't tell me which way to go unless you get what you want."

"The way out is that direction," Ben said, pointing to one of the tunnels. "I'll show you."

The president eyed Ben. "You don't negotiate very well, do you?"

For a few moments, the two men continued on in silence. Suddenly, the president spoke up. "Even if something like that really did exist, why do you actually think I'd just give it to you?"

Ben paused before answering. "Because, it will probably lead us to the discovery of the greatest Native American treasure of all time. . . . You're the president of the United States, sir, the highest office in the land. Whether by innate character, or to fulfill the oath of that office, or by the weight of history that falls upon you, I believe you to be the most just and honorable man in the country. I know you will make the right decision."

Shaking his head, the president sighed. "Gates, people don't believe that stuff anymore."

"But they want to believe it," Ben replied.

A short while later, in the forest surrounding Mount Vernon, a wooden door opened up through the dirt. Ben and the president crawled out and, after dusting themselves off, looked around.

"The nearest highway is that direction," Ben said, pointing. "You'll understand if we part ways here."

"That's it?" the president asked. Ben shrugged his shoulders. The president went on. "You risked your life to protect the Declaration of Independence. And for that, the following conversation never happened. The book exists."

From his wallet, the president pulled out a slip of paper. On the paper was a series of numbers. Ben was confused.

"Where else do you keep a book?" the president asked Ben. "The Library of Congress. XY234786."

"Thank you, sir," Ben said, smiling. He was still smiling when the president gave him the other numbers he would need in the library. When he had everything committed to memory, he began to walk away, but the president's voice stopped him.

"Two hundred people know you took me against my will," the president said, "and I can't tell them about the book." He watched Ben carefully. "You will be charged with kidnapping the president of the United States." Then the president grinned. "And Gates. Page one hundred seventy-four."

With an almost imperceptible smile, Ben nodded. Then he rushed off into the woods. Pushing through some bushes, he found his father waiting in his car. Climbing into the passenger seat, he flipped open his cell phone and began to dial.

"Riley," he said when his friend picked up, "meet us at the Library of Congress in twenty minutes."

CHAPTER FIFTEEN

It was late at night, but Agents Hendricks and Spellman knew their boss would want to hear the news. Calling him at home, they told him to meet them at Dr. Nichols's house.

"Neighbor found him a couple hours ago," Hendricks said as they walked into the academic's study.

On the floor was a body covered by a white sheet. Pulling it back, Spellman revealed Nichols and the gunshot that had killed him.

"He was the guy in charge of the Booth diary page," Spellman said. She watched as Sadusky viewed the body. His eyes fell to the man's hand. Dr. Nichols was wearing a Masonic ring.

Hendricks recognized that right away. "Hey," he said, "he's got a ring just like yours."

Just then, Agent Sadusky's cell phone rang. "This is Sadusky," he said into the phone. And then there was a pause. "The president's been . . . what?"

News of the president's disappearance—and its connection to Ben Gates—was now getting out to other law enforcement agencies. It was only a matter of time before Ben was caught.

Patrick was a nervous wreck. A short distance away, he sat at the wheel of his car while Ben, Riley, and Abigail snuck into the Library of Congress. He just hoped that they would find the president's book, and get out of there quickly.

Inside, Ben read the numbers the president had given him out loud. XY234786. The sequence didn't mean anything to Ben and Riley, but Abigail knew instantly.

"XY is a classification code," she explained, leading them through the library's rotunda. Taking a left, they almost ran into a librarian coming out of the secured door that led to the main stacks with a cart of books. Quickly, the trio slipped inside, moments before the door shut. Inside, they found themselves looking at floor-to-ceiling bookshelves lined with hundreds of books. But none of them had the XY sequence.

Moving to the second floor, the three scanned the books for the XY sequence. Suddenly, they found themselves looking at a door between two shelves. Ben knew just what to do. Punching in the code the president had given him, the door unlocked. They found themselves in a room overlooking the rotunda—and it was filled with XY books.

"Maybe someone checked it out?" Riley suggested when their search revealed no book matching the sequence perfectly.

Suddenly, Ben had an idea. Climbing up a ladder that rested against the shelves, he began pulling books out that were before and after the sequence. As Abigail and Riley looked on, Ben peered at the now empty shelf . . . and grinned.

"The numbers are a combination to a safe," Ben said triumphantly.

He spun the dial to 23-47-86 and then *click*—the panel popped open.

Back in Mount Vernon, agents ran down the tunnel, fanning out in all directions, searching for the president. But the president was far from Mount Vernon. He was on the side of the George Washington Memorial Parkway with cars and trucks blowing by him. It seemed that if he was going to get back to the White House, he was going to have to hitchhike. He stuck his thumb out hopefully.

A large eighteen-wheeler slowed and pulled over. It wasn't every day that the driver picked up a man in a tuxedo. The president climbed into the truck and asked for a phone. Eyeing his passenger carefully, the driver handed him his cell phone, saying, "Anyone ever tell you that you look like the president?"

Inside the library, Ben reached into the safe. Holding his breath, his fingers closed on something that felt very much like a book. Pulling out his hand, his face broke out into a wide smile. They had found the *Book of Secrets!*

Riley gasped. "I was right!"

Climbing down the ladder, Ben took the book and laid it on a desk. The thick book was stuffed with loose pages, and the binding cracked as Ben opened to the first page. George Washington's signature was penned on page one.

"Let's get to the good stuff!" Riley urged.

Ben carefully thumbed through pages with "Area 51" and "Kennedy Assassination" written on them, while Riley eagerly looked over his shoulder. Historical secrets were at their fingertips. He glanced at Ben, his eyes pleading. If he could just have a few moments with the book. . . .

"We don't have time," Ben said, catching his friend's look. He kept flipping pages until he came to an entry that read "City of Gold." A folded piece of paper was stuck in between the pages, and Ben took it out. It was an aged black-and-white photo of the plank that had once been in the Resolute desk in the Oval Office. It showed the remaining glyphs they needed.

"'1924. I found plank in secret desk compartment. Plank photographed and then destroyed,'" Ben read. Then he added, "'Borglum commissioned to destroy landmarks in Sacred Black Hills mountains.'"

"Borglum," Abagail interrupted. "Mount Rushmore?"

Ben nodded, realization dawning. "He carved Mount Rushmore in order to erase the landmarks."

Just then, police sirens wailed in the distance. "Go

to the car," he ordered. "I'll meet you there."

As the two took off, Ben quickly snapped a few photos of the book. There was someone who needed to see the remaining glyphs.

Abigail and Riley rushed through the Library of Congress. Dodging and weaving between the stacks of books, Riley couldn't help but notice that Abigaïl seemed pretty calm.

"How do you know where you are going?" he gasped.

Keeping her eyes forward, Abigail quipped, "I dated a librarian."

Taking another quick turn, the two found themselves staring at a service door. Throwing it open, they raced through, only to find two FBI agents, their guns drawn. Thinking quickly, Abigail held up her employee badge. "We were told to evacuate," she said calmly.

The two agents looked from Abigail's badge to Riley, back to the badge, and finally at Abigail. With a shrug, they nodded for them to pass. Then, not bothering to look back, the two agents darted into the building in search of Ben Gates.

★ ★ ★

While Abigail and Riley made their way toward the parking lot and their car, Ben was searching for his own way out. Unfortunately, he had ended up on the roof. Pulling out his cell phone, he dialed his father.

"Dad!" he cried when the older man picked up. "I'm sending a picture of the rest of the map to your phone. Take it to Mom. We need her to translate it."

On the other end of the line, one of the Wilkinsons listened in, intrigued by this latest development.

Unaware of the third listener, Patrick checked to make sure the photo had come through. When he had confirmed it, he started to hang up. But not before asking what Ben was going to do now.

"We're going to Mount Rushmore," Ben said. "Meet us there." Ending the call, he continued across the roof.

Suddenly, one of the doors burst open, revealing Agent Sadusky. Scanning the area, his eyes locked on Gates, who was stepping onto a ladder that led to another section of the roof. Quickly, Sadusky took off after him.

Unaware of the company, Ben headed to the far end of the building. Only, he soon found himself with nowhere to go but straight onto a rather fragile-looking stained-glass window.

"That's far enough, Ben," Sadusky said from behind him.

Turning, Ben saw the agent, his gun trained on him. Looking back at the glass, he took a step forward. Underneath his foot, the panel seemed to groan. Ben weighed his options. There was an FBI agent with a gun behind him, glass in front of him, and on his side . . . a ledge. Taking a deep breath, he ran and hurtled himself over the ledge. With a loud *thud*, he landed on another section of roof some fifteen feet below. Leaping to his feet, he took off . . . leaving an angry Sadusky behind.

Back in the parking garage, Abigail and Riley nervously waited for some sign of Ben. The longer they waited, the more chance they had of being discovered. Riley, his mind racing, fidgeted in his seat.

"So, let's recap," he said bitingly. "We've broken into Buckingham Palace, the president's desk, the Library of Congress, and kidnapped the president. What do we have to do next? T. P. the White House?"

In her seat, Abigail rolled her eyes. While Riley's

dramatics were amusing, she had to agree things were getting a little out of hand.

Suddenly, the driver's-side door opened and Ben slipped into the seat. With a smile at Abigail and Riley, he threw the car into gear and headed out of the lot— just as two agents burst into the garage. Seeing Ben at the wheel, the agents raced into their car and quickly took off after them. But luck was on Ben's side. Just as his car raced through the security gates, the guard on duty slammed a button. The hydraulic barriers meant to keep Ben from leaving, whooshed up moments *after* his car sped through. The agents, however, had no such luck. With a hiss, the barrier slashed into their car's tires, leaving them with four flats—and no Ben.

In her office at the University of Maryland, Dr. Emily Appleton was unaware of the trouble her son was in. She was just packing up to go home, when Mitch walked in, not bothering to knock.

"This office is closed," she said. "Office hours begin tomorrow at eight a.m."

"I do apologize for the late hour, Dr. Appleton," the man said. "My name is Mitch Wilkinson. I have something I need you to look at." Pulling out the phone he had been using to tap into Patrick's calls, he brought up the picture Ben had sent of the American half of the plank.

Emily looked at the phone and then eyed the stranger suspiciously. There was something about him that she didn't like. "You're a treasure hunter," she said by way of answering.

Mitch smiled. "No, ma'am. I'm a man looking to make his mark on history," he told her. Looking around the room, his eyes landed on another photo—this one of the plank taken in the queen's study.

Suddenly, Mitch's cell phone rang. Picking it up, he listened. When the caller had finished, Mitch hung up and gave Emily a stern glare. "Your ex-husband's on his way here. He wants the translation. Lie to him, get rid of him." He paused before adding, "His life depends on it."

CHAPTER SIXTEEN

As Ben, Abigail, and Riley successfully avoided capture and made their way to one of America's most recognizable landmarks, Patrick was on his way to the University of Maryland. Pulling onto the picturesque campus, he glanced at his watch and noted the late hour. He was sure that Emily would be in her office, so he quickly made his way there. "Emily?" he called, entering the empty office.

From behind him, Emily walked out of the copy room. "Patrick," she said, her voice chilly.

"Ben sent me—" Patrick began, pulling out his cell phone. Fumbling with the device, he tried to bring up the digital picture. Emily grabbed the phone and found the picture. "We know it leads to Mount Rushmore," Patrick said as his ex-wife examined the image.

"Islands of stone in a sea of grass," she said slowly. "That's what the Lakota used to call the Black Hills in South Dakota."

"What else?" Patrick asked eagerly.

Emily turned her attention back to the cell-phone screen. "Find where the moon touches the Earth," she translated, "and release the hummingbird." Then she handed the phone back to Patrick.

"That's it?" Patrick asked.

"It's never 'it,' Patrick," she scolded. "As a treasure hunter, you should know that."

This last comment was too much for Patrick to take. He had had enough. "Did it ever occur to you," he said, looking her straight in the eye, "and I can't believe that I'm saying this . . . that one reason I did what I did was in order to impress you?"

"Did it ever occur to you that I made sacrifices for us that *you* never did?" Emily said, holding his gaze. She watched how her words pained him, but she knew that she had no choice.

Patrick turned to exit, but before he did he thought to warn Emily of what she might soon hear.

"In the next few hours you might be seeing Ben on the news," he told her. "And not in a good way."

Emily looked a bit concerned, and then she laughed. "Well, it can't be any worse than stealing the Declaration of Independence."

Not answering, Patrick left. Emily watched from her office window as her ex-husband walked across the quad under the dim lamppost lights. While they were not on the best of terms, she hated that she had just lied to him. It put him—and Ben—in jeopardy.

"Don't feel bad," Mitch said, stepping up behind Emily. "Your son would've never found the treasure anyway."

"You don't know Benjamin," Emily said, her gaze not leaving the window.

"Perhaps not. But I have this." Pulling an aged letter out of his pocket, Mitch smiled. Even if Ben did figure out a way to decipher Emily's misleading clues, Mitch had the one piece of information Ben didn't. And without it, the glyphs were worthless. Holding the paper up, he pulled out a lighter and flicked it. The flame caught the page and it began to burn. Now he really was the only one who could find Cíbola.

CHAPTER SEVENTEEN

In the early morning light, the presidents' faces stood watch over the Black Hills of South Dakota. Inside Mount Rushmore's museum, Ben, Abigail, Riley, and Patrick stared out at the imposing facade. They were quiet as each of them pondered Emily's cryptic translation.

Abigail was the first to speak. "I haven't seen anything that even remotely resembles a hummingbird."

"Did Mom say anything else?" Ben asked after another few minutes. It felt like they were missing something obvious.

"She got a jab in about how she made sacrifices I didn't," Patrick said sullenly. For a moment, he looked like a little boy who had spilled his milk.

Ben, on the other hand, looked ecstatic. *"That's* where the hummingbird comes from. It was a story she used to tell me when I was little. It was an Aztec myth about the hummingbird, the god of sacrifice."

"She gave me a false clue and sent me on a wild goose chase?" Patrick asked in disbelief.

"But why that story?" Riley asked, once again feeling a bit confused.

"Because she was trying to tell us something," Ben answered. "The hummingbird sacrifices itself to protect its family, the Earth, and the Moon. . . ." His voice trailed off as he suddenly realized what his mother was protecting him from—Wilkinson! He must have been in the office when she was talking to Patrick. Grabbing his cell phone, Ben began to dial.

In the parking lot of a store not too far from the museum, Mitch sat in his SUV, guarding Emily. Suddenly her phone rang. Mitch smiled. Grabbing the phone out of Emily's purse, Mitch picked up.

"Hello, Dr. Gates," he said. "I had a feeling you would call."

On the other end of the line, Ben's hand tightened

around the phone. "Put my mother on," he snarled.

Holding the phone to Emily's ear, Mitch nodded at her. "Benjamin," Emily said, her voice calm, "there is a final clue to the treasure that only Wilkinson knows—" Before she could finish, Mitch pulled the phone back and flipped it shut. That should be enough information to send Gates running.

Back in the museum, Ben stared down at the now-silent phone. His mother was captured by a man intent on finding a treasure—no matter what the cost. Ben had no choice. He was going to turn himself in.

CHAPTER EIGHTEEN

Mitch, Daniel, and Seth made their way slowly up a trail weaving toward the top of Mount Rushmore, Emily between them. Through the trees, the faces of the presidents could be seen, staring down on the three criminals and their captive.

"We're never going to find a 'great cat' who 'guards an island of stone in a sea of trees' on this path," Seth complained, shifting his backpack from one shoulder to the other. Dr. Appleton had translated the glyphs correctly, but they seemed vague at best and completely insane at worst. Seth had very little faith that they were ever going to find the treasure.

Holding up a guidebook for his brothers to see, Mitch opened to a page that showed an old black-

and-white photo of the cliffs before they became Mount Rushmore. "Cougar Peak was destroyed during the first phase of construction," Mitch said in way of answer. "We've got to get to the highest point. This trail is the only way up."

The group continued to walk slowly upward. Suddenly, Agent Sadusky stepped out from behind one of the boulders that lined the path, his gun aimed straight at Mitch.

"You're a long way from home, Mitch Wilkinson," Sadusky said. Behind him, Spellman and two other agents stepped out from behind the trees, guns aimed at Daniel and Seth. "You are under arrest for the illegal capture and detention of Dr. Emily Appleton."

With a nod, the other agents descended upon the Wilkinson men, quickly cuffing them. When they were safely captured, Ben stepped out from behind another boulder and quickly rushed to his mother's side. "Are you all right?"

"I knew you'd figure it out!" Emily said, a proud smile on her face. Then she looked down and noticed that the Wilkinsons were not the only ones wearing handcuffs. Ben was too. "Oh, Ben. What did you do this time?"

Stepping up to Ben, Agent Sadusky answered for him. "Your son kidnapped the president of the United States." Noting the proud grin on Emily's face, Sadusky added, "Your boy does have certain skills, ma'am."

Emily agreed before turning back to the issue at hand. Mitch Wilkinson had the clue they needed if they were going to find a treasure.

Ben cleared his throat and looked at Sadusky. "I know I promised to cooperate, and I will, eventually, but—"

Sadusky didn't let him finish. "You're hardly in a position to make demands."

But Sadusky was wrong. "I took it," Ben said flatly.

For a moment, the agent looked disbelieving. But when Ben didn't back down, Sadusky ordered Seth and Daniel brought back down the mountain. Mitch would stay behind. Ignoring the confused looks of the other agents, Sadusky waited until they were gone before he spoke again. "Now tell me you did not take the president's book."

"Why don't you call him and ask?" Ben replied, knowing full well that Sadusky could do no such thing. It would implicate him in the entire thing and prove that he was a Mason. "I have to find the City of Gold. It's the only way to justify what I've done."

"If I let you go," Sadusky said after a pregnant pause, "how do I know you're going to tell me the truth about where the book is?"

"When you do let me go and I tell you where the book is, how long will it take before you catch me again?" Ben asked.

"About twenty minute. Maybe less."

Ben looked Sadusky straight in the eye. "So either way I'm caught, but this way you also get the book."

The man had a point. Sighing, Sadusky uncuffed Ben and gave him the keys to Mitch's. "The lookout, Harney's Peak," Ben said before turning and heading up the trail, Emily and Mitch with him.

Sadusky sighed. He had a detour to make.

As Sadusky was making his way to Harney's Peak, Ben, Mitch, and Emily were quickly making their way up the trail to the top of Mount Rushmore. After a few minutes, they met up with Patrick, Abigail, and Riley. They were all in hiking gear and appeared ready to go. His eyes falling on Emily, Patrick let out a relieved sigh. Despite their problems, he had never meant to get her into this mess. Riley, on the other hand, was not concerned with Emily. His eyes were locked on Mitch.

"I though the idea was to get him arrested," Riley said to Ben.

Not bothering to answer, Ben continued walking. They had ground to cover—and not much time to do it in.

Meanwhile, Agent Sadusky had made it to the Harney's Peak lookout. While the views were stunning, Sadusky didn't have time for such luxuries. He climbed the last steps and scanned the area for the book. In a corner, he found a plastic bag. Reaching in, he found Riley's, not the president's, book. Flipping it open, he found a note from Ben. It said: *"The book is safe. I told you that you could trust me. Ben."* Grumbling, Sadusky took his cell phone out and made a call.

"Notify the locals . . . police, rangers. I want Ben Gates found!" he snapped.

At that very moment, the man himself had just

made it to the highest point. Ben and the others stood on a rocky ridge overlooking a large lake. The water sparkled in the bright sun, making it look like one big inviting swimming pool. Clambering up the side of a rock that let him look further out, he scanned the area.

"Now all we gotta do is find the bird that sits on the crying dead guy," Riley said doubtfully.

"The bird sits on the warrior fallen in tears," Patrick clarified unhelpfully.

From his spot on top of the rock, Ben continued to look around. Suddenly, he spotted a stone jutting out into the lake. It looked just like a fallen warrior! "There!" Ben cried. "The tears are the lake!" Jumping down, he took off toward the stone, the others close behind.

But arriving at the stone, they found nothing that resembled a noble bird. They were at a dead end. Taking a step toward Mitch, Ben tried to stay calm. "All right, Wilkinson. What'd the letter say? What's the final clue?"

"Actually, there were three clues. If you take this off, I'll tell you," Mitch said, holding up his manacled hands.

"I'll consider it after you tell us," Ben said, not backing down.

Mitch saw the determination in Ben's eyes. He relented. "All right. 'The entrance shall only be revealed during a cloudless rain,'" he told them all.

Everyone looked up at the blinding sun. A lot of good that clue did them. "So . . . we come back when it's raining?" Riley asked.

"No," Ben said, concentrating. "Cloudless means you need the sun." He took off his backpack and rummaged around in it for a bottle of water. He opened the bottle and poured the water out on the granite. When the stone was wet, the color changed and the crystals in the rock sparkled.

"There it is!" Abigail cried, pointing to the now dampened stone. The water had revealed a secret etching. "It's an eagle!"

"The noble bird," Ben said, reciting the message his mom had translated, "will take your hand . . ."

"And give you passage," Emily finished.

Ben looked at the ground, his mind racing. What did they do now?

As if reading his thoughts, Mitch cleared his throat. "Well, we can all stand here and keep guessing, or I can tell you the answer." He held up his hands.

For a moment, Ben made no move. But finally, he released Mitch. They needed him, no matter the risk.

Rubbing his wrists, Mitch grinned. "'To awake the warrior, he must be nourished,'" he said.

"Nourished with what?" Abigail asked, confused.

Dropping to his knees, Ben examined the eagle. He started thinking out loud. "For the eagle to take one's hand . . ." he mumbled. The large eagle beak caught Ben's eye. "One must first offer it . . ." he said slowly. He touched the beak and noticed a thin crevice.

Carefully, he slipped his hand into the opening and then, slowly, his whole arm.

Thunk!

His audience gasped as his arm disappeared up to the shoulder! But Ben just smiled.

"It's a latch," he said. His face contorted as he pulled something the others could not see.

There was a scraping sound, and then one of the boulders nearby slowly rotated, creating an opening barely wide enough for one person to pass through. Beyond it, a tunnel of darkness was revealed.

Ben took a flashlight from his bag and ventured

into the dark passageway. The others followed.

Once inside, Ben flicked on the flashlight. The light beamed and showed an aged pulley system using thick vinelike ropes, logs, and boulder counterbalances.

"Ancient Aztec," Emily said. "Or Mayan."

"Same technology used to build the pyramids," Mitch added.

Outside, the telltale sound of a helicopter could be heard coming toward them.

"That one," Mitch said, pointing to one of the vine levers. "Before they find us!"

Patrick stepped forward. "No. We could end up trapped."

The sound of the helicopter grew louder and louder.

"On the other hand," Emily said, offering her opinion, "why build this passage and leave no way out?"

Surprised by Emily's astute comment, Patrick stared at her and then smiled. Abigail moved to the lever and, quickly getting group approval, she pulled the lever. The boulder entrance rotated closed. They were now engulfed in darkness, with just the single beam of light from Ben's flashlight to guide them.

Inside the helicopter, the agents looked at the

mountain and saw nothing but granite. They turned the helicopter and continued on with the search.

Ben pulled the lever again, but nothing happened. "Now we don't know how to get out," he said.

"Yeah, we do," Mitch said, pushing past the group. "Forward."

Riley sighed and mumbled to himself, "You haven't been on many treasure hunts, have you?"

The group moved slowly through the darkness until Ben's light shone on a stack of torches. Ben grabbed one.

"Anyone got a match?" he asked.

"I do," Mitch said.

Taking the matches, Ben quickly lit the torches. When everyone could see, they continued on through the narrow passage until they emerged in a cavern. The walls were covered with ancient murals and glyphs carved into the stone. Everyone stared in awe at the walls. This was the first time they had been seen in possibly hundreds of years.

Emily moved closer. In the torchlight, the murals seemed to come alive. She had spent her entire career teaching ancient languages and symbols. But now, her work, the real thing, was right in front of her.

Looking closer, she realized that the symbols and pictures told a story, an ancient prophecy.

"Pale gods will arrive in great ships, in search of gold," Emily said, translating aloud. "Cities will be destroyed." She looked to the others in disbelief. "This mural is at least three thousand years old," she said.

"The natives knew the conquistadors were coming?" Abigail asked in disbelief.

"So they hid their gold," Patrick said, realization dawning.

"Until today," Mitch chimed in.

"Only if we pick the right path," Riley added.

Everyone turned to Riley. He was looking at two openings. There was a straight path leading into darkness, but there was also a second path. Ben pointed his flashlight into the second path. The ceiling had collapsed and the way was littered with debris. The straight pathway was clear. It seemed the choice had been made for them.

"So who wants to go down the creepy . . . oh, forget it," Riley said, stopping himself. "I'll go first." This was beginning to feel awfully familiar—like when they found the Templar Treasure. Why was treasure always hidden in dark, creepy places? Riley wondered as he started walking down the dark path, the others following close behind.

For a while, there was no sound save the flickering flame and soft fall of footsteps. And then, the silence grew thicker as they realized that they had reached a dead end. In front of them was a solid rock wall with a hole carved in the stone. In that small spot there was an Aztec idol, its shiny body reflecting the torchlight.

"Gold!" Riley shouted.

Taking a step forward, Ben reached out his hand as if he were about to pick up the idol. But just then, Mitch pushed past Abigail and Riley. He wanted that idol. There was no way he'd let Ben get his hands on it. But as Mitch moved closer to the idol, something started to happen. The stone beneath their feet tilted forward. The extra weight had triggered a hidden system, and now the end of the floor closest to the idol began to tilt down, revealing a trapdoor. Bringing up the rear, Patrick and Emily watched as the floor opened up. Quickly, Patrick grabbed Emily and jerked her back. But Mitch, Ben, Abigail, and Riley all slid down and dropped out of sight.

Scrambling to the edge, Patrick called out, "Ben,

are you all right?" Peering down, he saw that the four were now standing on a round piece of stone.

"Mom! Dad!" Ben called up. "We'll come for you."

The trapdoor began to shift again, closing up the space between Ben and his parents. Within moments, the door slipped back to its original spot, leaving the two groups firmly separated.

Patrick and Emily looked at each other.

"It looked like they were all right," Patrick said, reassuring Emily. But she was not listening. She was moving toward the gold idol—just as Ben had done moments before. "Emily, what are you doing?"

"Get over here!" Emily ordered. They both tried to jump on the rock to make it move again, but their combined weight wasn't enough to do it. "So, I guess we try the other way," she said.

Patrick and Emily took the torches and walked back and stood in front of the second opening—the one they hadn't taken because it was filled with debris.

"Maybe it's safer to just wait," Emily said, looking at the littered passage.

"If they need help, we can't do much standing

here," Patrick told her. "That's our son down there." He moved closer to the opening.

Emily watched Patrick and couldn't help but be impressed. She joined him, and together they started to move the stones from the caved-in passage. It was hot and dirty work, and after a while Emily took off her suit jacket, revealing a light camisole. Glancing up from his lifting, Patrick felt his breath catch. Emily looked beautiful. He stood frozen, looking at her.

"What's wrong?" Emily asked, alarmed. "Are you all right?"

"Huh?" Patrick asked.

"Is the stone heavy?" she said, pointing to the stone in his hand.

"Uh-huh," he said.

"Why don't you put it down?" Emily suggested.

Patrick quickly put the stone down and carried on with the clearing, hoping that she hadn't figured out what had made him stop.

When Emily looked up again a while later, she saw Patrick squeezing through the small hole that they had cleared. He turned toward Emily, waving his torch.

"It's clear!" he called.

They moved forward and saw a staircase carved into the stone. It looked steep—and endless.

They just had to hope that the steps would lead them to Ben.

CHAPTER NINETEEN

On the other side of the trapdoor, Mitch, Ben, Abigail, and Riley stood staring at each other. They were on the circular rock that shifted each time some-one moved. Ben and Mitch tested the stability by stepping forward, but each had to quickly counterstep so the rock would not tilt. Finally, the four stepped to the edges of the rock and stood at an equal distance from one another. The rock was balanced—for now. Looking around, Ben searched for a way out.

Suddenly, Abigail let out a cry. "I see a rope!"

Sure enough, there was an old rope hanging down, and above it they could make out another ledge with what looked like a way out. But before they could do anything, Mitch reached for the rope, causing the rock to tip precariously.

"Mitch, no!" Ben cried.

"Sorry, Ben," Mitch said, trying to stay balanced. "If anybody's getting their hands on the rope, it's me."

"We have to work together here," Ben pleaded. "Or we won't survive."

But Mitch wasn't interested. He continued to move toward the rope, forcing Ben to step back to keep the rock balanced. Finally, Mitch reached out and grabbed the rope.

"Toss it over here," Ben said. Pointing to the ledge above, he added, "There's a notch. I think the rope can reach it. Wilkinson, throw me the rope."

In the torchlight, Mitch's smile looked wicked. "No," he said. "Even if it reaches, we can't all make it. The last person left is dead. That's not going to be me."

As his words sank in, the others looked at one another. Mitch was right. One of them would most likely die. But who . . .

Ben took a menacing step forward, his eyes locked on the rope. The rock tilted and Abigail and Riley scurried to balance it.

Suddenly, Abigail's voice echoed in the chamber. "I'll stay behind," she said calmly. She took a step back so that the rock tilted her way.

"No, I'll stay," Riley said. "You don't need me." He stepped back, balancing Abigail.

Ben looked at Abigail, his eyes full of unspoken emotion. "I am not leaving you behind."

"And Riley," Riley added, staring at Ben. He tried to help Ben by coaching him with his next sentence. "I'm not leaving you behind, *Riley*."

"Mitch," Ben said, "I'll stay behind. Take them with you."

"Sensible," Mitch said. Mitch reached out and grabbed the rope. Then he swung it up around the notch above him. He climbed up, leaving the remaining three to rebalance their weight to steady the rock. When Mitch reached the top, he took hold of the golden idol, unable to resist its lure.

"Is there a way out?" Ben called from down below.

It was too dark for Mitch to see anything. "I don't see one," he yelled. "Bring the flashlight!"

Carefully, Riley and Abigail climbed up the rope as Ben kept readjusting his weight to steady the rock. Finally, he stood alone in the dark, barely balanced in the center of the giant rock. He waited for an answer from Riley or Abigail.

On the ledge, Abigail stared at Mitch, who was still holding the idol. He was in a dream state, elated to have found the gold idol and completely unconcerned about Ben's situation.

"You know what this is?" Mitch asked. "Proof that my life means something."

Suddenly, Abigail knew what they needed to do. "It's nice," she said soothingly. "But it's not the City of Gold, is it?"

A moment later, Ben looked up to see the golden idol being lowered down to him by Abigail and Riley. Right away, he understood the plan. The idol would be able to balance the stone with its weight as he climbed up. But just as the idol was inches from the stone, the rope broke and the statue came crashing down. Ben scrambled and just managed to grab the end of the frayed rope as the rock fell into a deep abyss. He pulled himself up on the little bit of rope, and then, finally, on to the safety of the ledge.

"A sacrifice," Abigail explained. "We had to give up the idol in order to continue."

"Where's Wilkinson?" Ben asked, looking around.

The threesome turned toward the dark passage that had been revealed. Mitch was gone. And so was the flashlight.

The only light they had now was provided by the torch below. Ben looked disheartened. "We have to get the torch," he said.

"No, we don't," Riley said brightly. He dug into his pocket and pulled out a red, white, and blue glow necklace. He shrugged as Ben and Abigail stared at him. "Gift-shop impulse item," he said.

With the light from the necklace to guide them, Ben, Abigail, and Riley stepped into the corridor. They went down the path for a stretch in relative silence, each lost in their own thoughts. Suddenly, something up ahead started to twinkle like tiny stars in the night sky.

"Um . . . you guys seeing that?" Riley said.

Just then, the passage opened up, revealing an enormous cavern . . . and Mitch. The other man was clutching the flashlight, his eyes trained on the sight in front of him.

The giant cavern was sparkling. The high walls shimmered with gold, and a large waterfall spilled into a lake that covered the whole cave.

"The City of Gold!" Riley shouted.

"It's beautiful," Abigail said in awe.

But then Ben spoke. "It's pyrite," he said. "Fool's gold." He also pointed out that there was no city—just a lake.

Mitch came up behind them. "He's right."

Dejected, Ben sighed. "There is no City of Gold."

"And that's not even the bad news," Mitch said. "There's no way out of here." He pointed the flashlight to a skeleton wearing tattered clothing.

"Why would the natives design a labyrinth of fatal traps if they were hiding nothing?" Ben said. He looked at the waterfall, his eyes coming to rest on several stones. "Look at those crystals," he said, pointing. "The water level hasn't changed in here in hundreds of years. That's an awful lot of water coming in. Where is it going out?"

Ben took the flashlight from Mitch and aimed the beam into the lake. The light cut through the water. As he gazed into the water, something shiny caught Ben's eye. Underneath the water, the golden face of an ancient statue appeared.

"They hid their gold in the lake!" Riley shouted.

"Although it wasn't a lake when they hid it," Ben

said, correcting Riley. "They wouldn't hide gold somewhere they could never reach. The natives had sophisticated irrigation systems by the time the conquistadors arrived." Silently, Ben looked around. There had to be some tool, some way, to get to the gold. Just then, Ben noticed one of the stone formations appeared to be man-made. He waded over to it and realized—it was a stone wheel! "Help me turn it!" he yelled.

In another part of the underground cavern, Patrick and Emily carefully walked down a dark stairway. Unfortunately, they had just arrived at an impasse—or rather, a large chasm. Patrick looked over at Emily and then around the area. In the dim light from his torch, he could make out a chain hanging from a beam in the ceiling. Reaching out, he grabbed it. "I think we can make it," he said bravely. He pushed off and swung out. But not far enough. The chain swung back, and Emily reached out to help. But the force of the swing knocked her off balance. Grabbing her, Patrick pulled her to him. This time they swung safely across, landing on the opposite ledge with a *thud*.

After they had collected themselves, they continued down the stairs.

Suddenly, Emily gasped and stopped short. In her path was a skeleton dressed in colonial-era clothing. "One of the Roanoke colonists!" she cried, referring to the group of colonists who had vanished without a trace in the late fifteen hundreds.

Patrick looked ahead. "It looks like it's all of them," he said. He pointed farther down the steps where a dozen more skeletons in similar clothing were scattered. There was a great stone door covered in glyphs, marking the end of the staircase.

"They got trapped down here," Patrick said.

Emily pushed forward to the door. "They couldn't open the door."

"Can you?" Patrick asked, hoping that Emily's understanding of the ancient writing would be helpful.

"Yeah," Emily said, recognizing the symbols. "It should be here." She felt around for the doorjamb. When her hand slid into a hole, she let out another gasp. Then her fingers found a lever, and she grinned.

But her grin faded. "It's stuck," Emily told him.

Coming up beside her, Patrick nudged her aside.

He put his hand in the hole and pushed down.

"I think that I almost got it," Patrick said.

But there was something Patrick didn't know. On the other side of the stone wall, an entire lake's worth of water waited, ready to rush in.

On the ledge overlooking the lake, Ben was hard at work, trying to get the ancient wheel to turn. The others joined him. Finally the stone started to slowly move. Looking up, the group watched as two large boulders rolled in front of the waterfall and acted like a dam, keeping the water back. And then, right before their eyes, the water started to recede.

No one spoke as the water drained out of the cavern. They were standing on a ledge, high above the bottom of what had only moments before been a lake. Where the water had once been, there were now gigantic golden pyramids and statues that glinted and twinkled. They had found the City of Gold!

CHAPTER TWENTY

"Looks like we're rich . . . again," Riley said, staring at all the gold surrounding him. He knew that was an understatement. What he was staring at was priceless.

"This place is sacred. It isn't for anyone to own," Ben said softly.

Mitch stepped forward. "I'm glad to hear you feel that way," he said. "I really wasn't planning on sharing it." With that, Mitch shoved Riley, sending him toppling over the ledge.

Before Ben could reach Riley, Mitch swung his flashlight at Ben. But Ben was too fast, and he ducked, grabbing Mitch's wrist and then slamming it into the wall.

While the two men fought, Abigail ran to the edge and looked over. Riley was holding on to the ledge for dear life. Meanwhile, Mitch had recovered from his wrist being slammed and now turned to face Ben. It was an intense match as the two men swung at each other atop the precariously high ledge. Mitch gathered strength and lunged at Ben, knocking him over. Ben's fighting instincts were sharp, and he grabbed Mitch's ankles. Mitch went down, his momentum carrying him over the edge. But as he slipped off he reached out and took hold of Abigail's arm!

"Abigail!" Ben screamed. He moved quickly and reached out to catch her arm before she could go over the edge with Mitch. As Ben pulled her up to safety and hugged her tight, Mitch plunged down into the jagged rocks far below.

Meanwhile, Riley managed to pull himself up and collapsed, catching his breath. He reached for the flashlight and beamed the light in front of him, catching sight of Ben and Abigail . . . hugging. They were no longer the picture of a feuding, broken-up couple, that was for sure. Then in the corner of his eye, Riley caught sight of something.

"Look!" he shouted.

Ben and Abigail pulled apart and looked over at Riley.

"A staircase," Riley said, pointing.

Patrick grunted and shifted his weight. He tried the latch again, and this time the stone door *moved*. As the door opened, water gushed in at a whirling speed. Patrick grabbed Emily, and they held tight against the rising water. But the water level didn't rise above their ankles! Feeling elated, they both looked toward the golden light coming through the doorway. Together, they walked through it and stared in awe at the sight before them.

"The City of Gold!" Emily exclaimed.

Patrick hung his head. "It means nothing without Ben," he said, his voice filled with worry.

"Mom! Dad!"

Turning, Emily and Patrick watched as their son, a triumphant look on his face, raced down a long staircase. Reaching them, he embraced both of them in a strong hug.

A while later, Ben, Patrick, Emily, Abigail, and Riley found themselves on the granite plateau where it all started. With a sigh, Ben took out his cell and made a call. It was time to set things right.

"Are you ready to turn yourself in?" Agent Sadusky asked on the other end of the line. He was at the Mount Rushmore parking lot surrounded by a couple of dozen agents.

"Not quite," Ben told him. "Tell the president that I want to talk to him."

Sadusky laughed. "That's not going to happen."

"We found the City of Gold," Ben said.

The agent paused. He was impressed. And awed. The ancient city did exist. "It doesn't matter," he told Ben. "You still committed a federal crime."

Ben was prepared for that response. "I may not have taken the book, but that doesn't mean I didn't see what's in it. I know what's on page one hundred seventy-four." There was complete silence on the phone. "Sir?" Ben asked.

"Gates," Sadusky finally said. "You think that the president is going to care?"

"This one?" Ben asked. "He'll care."

A while later, Agent Sadusky stood next to Ben and looked out in wonder at the City of Gold.

Behind them, the others looked on in silence.

"I can't believe you really found it," Sadusky said to Ben. "Too bad no one can ever know about it."

"But this is an amazing discovery!" Abigail piped up, unwilling to stay quiet.

"We found the Roanoke colonists!" Emily argued.

Sadusky shook his head. "The president has his reasons." Then he paused. "Don't worry. You will all be credited with your discoveries."

"Yeah, in a book that no one knows or will ever know exists," Riley said, moping a little.

"The president has agreed to give you all a reward," Sadusky said. "I don't know what's on page one hundred seventy-four, but it must be a doozy."

Riley watched as two agents emerged from the tunnel carrying something shrouded in a Masonic apron. "Hey, what's that?" he asked Sadusky.

"What's what?" Sadusky asked innocently. The agents nodded at him as they walked past.

Suddenly, things started to make sense to Ben. "That's really why you told me about the book, isn't it?"

The veteran agent smiled coyly at Ben. "What book?"

★ ★ ★

The orange and violet light of the South Dakota sunset cast a warm glow over Mount Rushmore. Carrying a bag of popcorn, Ben made his way over to his seat. All around, people were looking at the monument, ready for the night's fireworks show. Ben passed his parents, locked in an embrace and kissing. He stopped, stunned.

"You know, son, the best thing about arguing is making up," Patrick said when he caught Ben staring.

"And we have a lot of making up to do," Emily said.

"I'll never get used to that," Ben mumbled.

His parents laughed and Ben continued on his way and found his seat . . . next to Abigail. He handed her the popcorn and a drink.

"Thanks," she said softly. "So, about the tea tables . . ."

"I'll have the movers bring them to you next week," Ben told her, getting back to their earlier disagreement about splitting up their furniture.

"I was going to say you can keep them. . . ." Abigail said. She watched Ben's smile fade. She grinned at him before adding, "And then move back in with me?"

Ben's face lit up as he looked deep into the eyes of the woman he loved. Pulling her close, they melted into a passionate kiss, while in the sky above, fireworks went off. Pulling away, Abigail smiled, and Ben knew—that was worth more than all the gold in the world.

The End

Benjamin Franklin Gates is only the latest in a long line of treasure hunters. Go back to the beginning of America's history and discover how the Gates family's quest began in Changing Tides.

Changing Tides

A Gates Family Mystery

★ ★ ★

By Catherine Hapka

Based on characters created for the theatrical motion picture "National Treasure"

Screenplay by Jim Kouf and Cormac Wibberley & Marianne Wibberley

Story by Jim Kouf and Oren Aviv & Charles Segars

LONDON, 1612

"**W**here are you off to then, son?"

Samuel Thomas Gates paused at the threshold of his family's flat. His father was smiling at him from the doorway of the back room. Dressed only in breeches and a half-fastened linen shirt, Benjamin Gates's thin shoulders stooped, his pale brown hair was messy, and flecks of that morning's meal dotted his untrimmed beard. He held a metal escapement in one hand and a clock casing in the other. While it was a holiday and the shops were closed, Benjamin was a clockmaker by avocation as well as by trade.

Even in his off-hours, he liked nothing better than tinkering with the intricate innards of one of his timepieces.

Since turning eighteen earlier that year, Sam sometimes had the unsettling feeling of peering into a looking glass when facing his father. They were now of equal height, and except for a few extra wrinkles around the father's eyes and a bit less hair at the temples, looked much alike.

"I'm going to the theater, Father," Sam said, adding quickly, "I have the sixpence to pay my way—a gentleman gave me it as a tip at the shop last week."

Benjamin laughed. "No need to worry about that, my lad. If things go as I think they shall, you'll soon be able to attend the theater every day if you so wish. And be seated in a fine box, no less." He gave a broad wink. "What is the play today?"

Sam was glad to see his father in such good spirits. Benjamin had been hinting lately of a mysterious financial windfall, though the rest of the family knew better than to ask too many questions. Sam only hoped he was aiming to sell one of the finely crafted clocks he'd been working on to a wealthy gentleman, rather than hoping—yet again—to procure a fortune through some harebrained scheme. Benjamin Gates was one of the cleverest men Sam knew, as well as one of the kindest, but he could be troublingly naive in matters of money. That was one reason why the flat's furniture was threadbare and the family's clothes patched over and over until they fell apart entirely.

"It is the latest by Mr. Shakespeare," Sam answered. "*The Tempest*, I believe he calls it. I know little of the plot, but I did enjoy his *Macbeth* when I saw it performed last year."

Benjamin smiled broader and dropped a hand on Sam's shoulder. "I suppose it matters not what the play is, eh, so long as the company is agreeable?" He winked again. "Will young Miss Sarah Moore be attending, do you suppose?"

Sam felt his cheeks blush crimson. It shouldn't have come as a surprise that his father was aware of Sam's affections. Benjamin had a head for puzzles and mysteries and secrets of all kinds. Not only could he fix any clock or other mechanical device there was, but he enjoyed working codes and could guess the ending of nearly any book or play before it was half over. Which meant, keeping secrets around him was a rather difficult task.

"I had best be off," Sam said hurriedly, not bothering to answer his father's question. "I'll want to arrive early to find myself a proper spot in the yard near the stage."

"Get along with you, then," Benjamin said, cuffing him good-naturedly on the shoulder. "Have a fine time at your theater."

"Thanks, Father." Sam hurried out the door and onto the street outside, humming under his breath all the while. He barely noticed the familiar sights, sounds, and smells of the city, or paid any mind as he dodged two dogs fighting noisily in the street. His father had seemed pleased by the idea that Sam might fancy Sarah Moore. That was a relief;

Sam had feared he might disapprove of such a match. After all, her family was much better off than their own.

Then again, why should Father disapprove of such a thing as that? Sam thought as he waited for a four-in-hand to trot past before continuing across the street. *It is what he did himself—married a woman well above his station. And Mother says she has never regretted a moment of it.*

He smiled fondly as he thought of his mother, Alice, toiling on in the modest flat without complaint, stretching every penny as far as it would go. Though Benjamin had always managed to eke out a modest living with his clocks, he could be too much the perfectionist and rather slow, which meant that money was always tight. True, Sam and his elder brother, William, did what they could to help. Sam was apprenticed at a bookbinder's shop, and William brought in a steady, though modest, income as a laborer. So things weren't *too* terrible. Perhaps it was time to broach the subject of an official courtship. After all, Sam was eighteen now—more than man enough to strike out on his own.

Of course, marriage to a humble shopboy may not please Sarah's father, even if she is willing to take me as I am, he thought with a twinge of anxiety. *If only there were a way to pay for a real education, I know I could make much of it. . . .*

His gaze flickered over to a nearby building and landed on a familiar broadsheet hanging on the side. The Virginia Company had been advertising all over London for would-be colonists, promising volunteers a share in the riches of the New World across the ocean. Sam had heard the tales William had brought back from the docks—tales of gold gleaming out from every bit of rock, jewels tumbling in upon the shore with the ocean waves, even precious minerals dripping from the trees.

For a moment he drifted to a stop in front of the broadsheet, contemplating what he could do with such wealth. First of all, he would be able to attend Oxford. There he could study history, Greek, astronomy, and more. For as long as he could remember, Sam had burned to know more of the larger world outside the few humble London blocks that made up his own entire existence. His mother, who had received more education than many ladies, had taught him to read and write as a small boy, and he took whatever spare time he had to read the books that passed through the shop. Books by learned and worldly men of the day, such as Sir Walter Raleigh, John Donne, Captain John Smith, the late Christopher Marlowe, and even the brand-new English translation of the great novel of the Spaniard, Cervantes, among others. Sometimes he felt as if he would never have time enough to read all he would like.

But all that would be different if he had even a small share of those New World riches. What's more, as a wealthy, educated man he would be able to court Sarah in the way she deserved. He would be able to afford a horse and carriage, a fine house for his whole family, all the clock parts his father could want, and a staff of servants, including a maidservant whose only task would be to wait on his weary mother's every need.

After a moment he sighed and moved on, chiding himself for such foolish daydreams. What did one such as he know of such fortune-hunting? He was no stout and sturdy adventurer. He was merely a shop boy, pale of skin and rather weak of limb—as burly William delighted in proving in his frequent challenges to impromptu wrestling matches.

And then there was Sarah herself. Though Sam had heard that girls and women were now among the colonists in the New World, he couldn't imagine Sarah among them, with her fine clothes and love of the theater. And she had many admirers—if he went off to the New World without her, it seemed quite unlikely that she would still be waiting for him when he returned.

No, it was madness to think of such things—that sort of dreaming was what always earned his father snickers from the neighbors. He should try to be more like William, who seemed perfectly content in his simple life of hard labor, deep sleep, and a nip of strong ale in between.

Soon Sam reached the Globe Theater, its three-story octagonal walls and the thatched roof covering the galleries towering grandly over its neighbors in the rather lowbrow Southwark district along the Thames. Sam paid his admission and made his way to the crowded pit in front of the raised stage, where he jostled for position among the sailors, laborers, and miscellaneous groundlings who had gathered for an afternoon at the theater. His shoes crunched on the hazelnut shells underfoot as he found a spot only a few bodies back from the edge of the stage. Several members of the actors' company were busy arranging props upon the stage for the coming performance.

"Look!" a man standing nearby shouted, pointing at the stage. "Isn't that Mr. Shakespeare himself?"

"It is!" another playgoer cried out. "Oi! Oi! Playwright!"

A number of others nearby began calling out and tossing hazelnuts at the slight, bearded figure on the stage. The playwright scurried out of range and cursed at them irritably, causing much laughter among the groundlings. Sam watched as Mr. Shakespeare bustled off with the other members of the company. But he was less interested in the celebrated writer and actor than in someone else.

Turning away from the stage, he raised his eyes to the lowest level of roofed galleries above, searching for a certain familiar face. He smiled when he spotted it. Sarah was sitting with her sisters, looking like a china doll with her pale skin and hair, her heart-shaped face framed by her high collar and lace bodice. After a moment she must have felt his gaze. Meeting his eyes, she wriggled her fingers in a wave. He waved back vigorously.

"Watch it, mate," the man beside him grumbled, giving him a shove as Sam accidentally bumped him.

But Sam hardly noticed. Just seeing Sarah had lifted his spirits. The Gates family might not be wealthy, but it was hardworking and respectable. Surely Sarah's father would come to appreciate that.

In any case, Sam was determined that it was indeed time to make his intentions known and come what may.

Sam was still in a good mood as he walked home after the play. The performance had been a fine one, filled with humor and drama. Sam found it a wonder that it had been written by a man so much like an older version of himself. Hadn't Mr. Shakespeare, too, come from humble beginnings? Didn't he, too, lack much in the way of formal education?

And yet look what a life he has made for himself here in London, Sam thought as he walked. *All from a deep love of words and the theater. If only Father's love of timepieces could make him as well off as that, or my interest in books and knowledge . . .*

His thoughts were interrupted by a great shouting from the flat just ahead. It was William's voice, and he sounded as angry as Sam had ever heard him, though he couldn't make out his words. Sam put on speed, wondering if his brother had surprised a thief in their home—for what else could rouse William's even temper?—and burst into the flat.

"What is it?" he cried. He glanced around for the thief or other interloper, but saw only his family gathered in the main room. William's broad, handsome face was bright red beneath its shock of black hair. Benjamin stood before him in silence, looking small, pale, and slight before his brawny eldest son. Alice Gates was nearby, her face streaked with tears.

"Samuel," Alice cried when he entered. "Oh, Samuel!"

"What is the matter?" Sam asked, his heart racing. "William, why are you shouting?"

William strode toward him, his expression so dark and angry that Sam took a half step backward. "Ask him!" William roared, jabbing a finger in their father's direction. "He's the one who has ruined the Gates name!"

Benjamin raised both hands before him. "Please, son," he began weakly. "I thought this would help all of us. How was I to know that man was a charlatan? He seemed most sincere."

"Father?" Sam's body went cold as he recalled Benjamin's earlier comments about money. "What have you done?"

Between Benjamin's stuttering and William's shouting, he soon had the answer. Unbeknownst to any of them, Benjamin had invested in an expedition to the New World. He had used not only all of the very modest Gates fortune, but had also borrowed from several wealthy customers to raise the money required by the man he'd met at the local pub. This man had led him to believe that he would be sponsoring a group of adventurers who would bring back riches beyond imagining . . .

". . . like the riches found by the Spanish not long ago," Benjamin finished, his eyes distant.

William shook his head, still scowling. "Instead, the

charlatan disappeared, never to be heard from again," he spat out. "He took our money and ran. Riches beyond imagining, all right. Enough for that scoundrel!"

"But how do you know he is a scoundrel?" Sam's mind jumped back to that broadsheet with its promise of untold wealth. "Could the expedition be real?"

William shot him a look of disgust. "You sound like Father."

Sam shrank back. He knew his father was a dreamer, impractical verging on foolish. But was he, himself, really the same, with his dreams of education and a bright future? Is that how his brother viewed him? Is that how *others* viewed him?

"It is not real, Sam," Benjamin said quietly. "William has learned the truth from an acquaintance just this day."

"I wager this puts an end to your wasting money on plays and books and such, little brother," William snapped, his voice dripping with disapproval.

"Yes," he said slowly. This had not been one of his father's usual small schemes, risking just a few pounds here or there. This was different. "I guess it's the end of all such pleasures."

Benjamin turned to Sam, despair in his eyes. "I did it for all of us, Sam. Can you see that?" he said. "I was going to send you to university . . ."

Sam wanted to do as he'd done time and again—to smile and say it was all right, that they would muddle through somehow. But how could he? His father had ruined them all—and their family name. It was one thing to be a pauper; quite another to be known as a debtor and a fool.

"Sam?" Benjamin pleaded. "My boy?"

His heart breaking, Sam shook his head and turned away to escape his father's eyes. There was nothing to say.

Sarah will never look at me again once she hears of this, he thought. *The name Gates will be spoken with nothing but mockery, and I shan't be able to show my face anywhere in London. I'll be lucky if Mr. Wesley will still have me at the shop once the wags start with their gossip.*

He glanced at his irate brother and his weeping mother, who hadn't said a word since his arrival. No, this mistake would not soon be fixed.

Risking a quick glance at his father, he saw that Benjamin had his head in his hands. Sam quickly looked away again. His father was so good at guessing the outcome of the plots of silly novels and plays. So how could he be so terrible at it in real life?

The adventure continues in
Changing Tides
available wherever books are sold.